AMONG THE STARS

THE ACCIDENTAL ASTRONAUT

MATTHEW K WYERS

REFLECT LIGHT PUBLISHING

Book Cover Design by ebooklaunch.com

❀ Created with Vellum

This work is dedicated to my long time friends:

Jimmy Dockery and Lara Eide

Without your encouragement, I never would have taken writing seriously.

Rest in peace my friends.

SIGN UP FOR INFO ON MATTHEW K WYERS

To get info on the latest releases, sign up for the newsletter, or follow Matthew's blog.

Go to:

https://www.matthewkwyers.com

We are not alone.

CHAPTER 1

"YOUNG MAN, what type of person do you want to be?" The principal leaned over his desk and peered at the alleged troublemaker.

Micah Alfero raised his head and made eye contact. "My father was an astronaut and all I ever wanted was to be just like him."

"If that's what you wanted then perhaps you should have stayed in the Junior Star Force program," replied the principal. "As it is, you've chosen to enter our school and apply yourself to academic prep, but you don't seem to understand that there's no adventure to be had here. There'll be no antics from little kids pretending to be heroes and there's certainly no room for anyone who picks fights."

"Sir, I didn't pick a fight. I was trying to protect Hannelore," Micah said.

The principal huffed and straightened his back. "Ms. Allbrooks is perfectly capable of taking care of herself. If you see anyone acting out of line with the code of conduct, then you should report that immediately to a teacher or a supervisor. You do not take matters into your own hands. Do I make myself clear?

"Yes sir," replied Micah.

The principal pointed at Micah. "You come highly recommended by the Star Force commandant, but I don't care. Anymore episodes like this from you and you'll be expelled. Is that understood?"

"Yes sir," replied Micah.

"You can go," the principal sat back down and dismissed the boy with a wave of the hand.

Micah got up and left the principal's office.

Outside waiting for him was Hannelore, the girl who had captured Micah's 12-year-old heart without knowing it.

"Hi, I'm Hannelore." She extended her hand.

Micah looked at the floor. "Yes, I know."

Hannelore cocked her head to the side. "Huh?"

His eyes widened after hearing his own dumb words. "I mean, hi, I'm Micah. Micah Alfero."

"You live down the street, don't you?" Hannelore said.

"Yeah, we just moved in last month," Micah replied.

"Well, I wanted to thank you." Hannelore bit her lip.

Micah smiled. "Oh, it's no problem. I don't like bullies and that Travis kid is a real jerk."

"Yeah, he is. He's been picking on me since last year, but he's never pushed me down like that. I wasn't sure what to do." Hannelore smiled back.

"Maybe he'll leave you alone now that all the teachers know what's been going on," Micah said.

Hannelore swung her arms. "Um...ya know, what you did was really cool. I mean, I know he kind of flattened you after you punched him, but I still thought it was pretty brave."

Micah turned red. "At least I got the first shot in, I guess."

Hannelore nodded. "Your only shot."

"Yeah, thanks for reminding me," Micah shrugged.

"I'm just kidding with you." Hannelore laughed. "I heard you came from Cape Canaveral."

Micah shuffled to his side. "Yeah, my family is originally from here so my mom and I moved back."

Hannelore leaned in a little. "Oh, what about your dad?"

Micah stiffened up. "Oh...he died."

"I'm sorry. I shouldn't have asked," Hannelore said.

"It's ok." Micah looked to the ground again. "Well, I better get going. Mom will wonder why I'm late coming home."

"It was nice to meet you Micah. Maybe we should hang out sometime," Hannelore glanced away.

"Yeah, that would be great!" Micah's eyes widened again. "I mean, that's cool."

And hang out they did. Over the next couple of months, Micah and Hannelore became great friends. They told each other their stories, their secrets, and what they wanted to be when they grew up one day.

One evening, the two pre-teens sat in the park just down the street from their neighborhood.

A few kids were playing soccer in the distance and there was a nice Summer breeze in the air.

It was a little quiet though as both Hannelore and Micah had run out of things to say.

"You never told me what happened to your dad," Hannelore said. "You don't have to tell me, but I was just curious."

Micah rubbed his knees. "You ever heard of the Star Cruiser?"

"Yeah, I think everyone has," replied Hannelore.

Micah looked away. "My dad helped build it. He spent most of his life in space flying shuttles. After the shuttle missions ended, he went into engineering. He was brilliant, one of the country's best scientists. He wanted to help mankind fly farther and faster than ever before. Humans would visit another solar system and see what there was to see. I was so proud of him. My dream was to follow in his footsteps, to be an astronaut and travel the stars. When I was ten years old, he got me enrolled in the Junior Star Force program. I was a good student too. I learned how to fly antique spacecraft, advanced astronomy, and physics… nothing was all that hard for me. Everything was going great there for a couple of years."

Hannelore crinkled her nose. "I don't understand. What happened?"

"The day of the launch came. My mother and I went down to the Cape to watch. It was a clear March day. The stadium near the launch site was full to the brim. Over 100,000 people had bought tickets to see it. And because my dad was on the flight team, we had the best seats in the house." Micah had a tear in his eye.

Hannelore frowned. "Your dad was on board?"

"When the rockets fired, it was beautiful. I had seen launches before, but I was really young then and I didn't appreciate them. Now, I could see the whole sky fill up with smoke and fire. And sitting on top of it all was my dad, but something went wrong. As the ship neared orbit, they fired up the star drive and something exploded. The crowd gasped and then the entire ship blew up. I don't remember much else about that day." Micah sniffled.

Hannelore's shoulders sunk. "I'm so sorry."

"Within a few weeks, they found some wreckage. They found the bodies of the other pilots. They never found my dad though," Micah said.

Micah didn't say much more about it, but as the sun was setting on another day with his newfound friend Hannelore, he heard a faint bark.

Just a few feet behind them stood a mutt of a dog if there ever was such a thing. Long-haired with big eyes, he was gray with a little brown mixed in.

"Where did you come from you little goob?" Hannelore gleamed.

The dog barked again and if one could speak 'canine' as some believe they can then one would have understood this mutt as saying something like "hello, I'd like to be your friend."

Hannelore jumped up to stroke the mutt on his head. "I've always liked dogs. They're goofy and goofy things make life worth living. That's my philosophy."

"Mom never wanted us to have any pets. She's not allergic so I don't know why," Micah said.

The little mutt crawled up under Micah's arm and sat for a moment. Then he popped up and licked Micah on the chin only to sit back down and look satisfied with himself.

"Oh, that's nasty! You slobbered!" Micah tried to dry the slobber with the tail of his shirt.

"Ok, I know my dad won't allow a dog in the house so you take him home and beg your mom to keep him. Sound like a plan?" Hannelore smiled.

"My mom will never go for that," Micah rolled his eyes.

"Trust me. Things might be different now that..." Hannelore shut her mouth.

"Different now that...what?" Micah scratched the mutt's back.

"Just trust me," Hannelore implored. "Give him a name and take him home. He doesn't have a collar so we know he doesn't belong to anyone. This way we'll get to keep him."

"I could call him Jimmy. That was my dad's name," Micah stood up to head back home.

"Yeah, I think that's nice. I'll see you tomorrow." Hannelore bounced to her feet.

"Will do," Micah replied.

"And call me if your mom doesn't go for it. I'll beg my dad and maybe he'll cave." Hannelore waved.

Micah ran for home hoping to get the dog to play along.

It worked just fine as Jimmy, the mutt, followed.

"Dogs can't resist chasing a kid running, I swear." Micah laughed.

Micah's mother Elizabeth swung open the door once she saw Micah running for home. "What in the world's the matter?"

"Found a dog!" Micah pumped his fist.

"Oh mercy, you scared me. I thought something bad might have happened," Elizabeth pursed her lips.

"No, mom...I just wanted him to...um...follow me home." Micah's eyes zeroed in on the ground.

Elizabeth put her hands on her hips. "Son, you know how I feel about dogs. They're so dirty and so much trouble and they poop on the carpet for heaven's sakes. What sort of creature does that and hops off on their merry way?"

Micah gulped and enacted the plan. "I named him Jimmy...after dad."

Elizabeth teared up. "You shouldn't have done that."

"I'm sorry mom. I didn't mean to upset you," Micah said.

Elizabeth wiped her eyes. "No, it's ok. Keep the dog for now. I think it would be nice to hear that name around the house again."

"Thanks mom," Micah said as he slipped her a quick hug and walked inside the house.

The mutt followed them inside and jumped on the couch the first chance he could get.

The evening waned and Micah once again laid in a bed that still didn't quite feel like his own although this time Jimmy, the mutt, slept at the foot.

"Goodnight Jimmy. We'll get you a collar in the morning." Micah dozed off.

He dreamed the same thing he dreamed almost every night. He remembered all the toughest things that happened after the accident. In his dreams, it was as if he hovered above the events and relived them over and over again.

Micah saw the graveyard. The time had come for the funeral. There was no corpse to bury, but there was a ceremony just the same. The boy who had just lost his father, stood silently. He gazed on with his brown eyes as an empty casket lowered into the ground.

He was an only child and, on this day, was the only comfort for his mother.

She buried her face into his dark brown hair as they both cried profusely. With all the rain though, it was impossible to see the tears.

They were wearing black as was the custom. They stood overlooking a family plot at the old Garden City Church. Most of the graves were from a hundred years ago or more. The headstones stuck out of the ground like monuments to a bygone era.

A priest presided over the service and did his best to give the family comfort, but they had none.

"May the Lord bless you and keep you," said the priest.

"Thank you," said Elizabeth.

With that, the funeral ended and Micah desperately wanted his life to be normal again, but there was no going back. He had the opportunity to continue with the Junior Star Force program, but didn't want to be a part of it anymore.

Micah's own words echoed through the dream. "Space killed my father. I want nothing to do with it."

Every morning, Micah woke up with a fresh remembrance of all the tragedy.

He and his mother had moved back to Garden City so they could be free of any reminders of the space program at Cape Canaveral. They tried to move on with life, but it was an impossible task.

Before his father was lost aboard the maiden voyage of the Star Cruiser, Micah was a normal boy with quite an outgoing personality. After that day, however, he was reserved, timid, and cynical.

But now that Hannelore had come along, things looked brighter.

Hannelore was nerdy, cute without a doubt, but awkward as any 12-year-old is. She had blonde hair, blue eyes, and wore pink braces. One might describe her as a girly girl, but one would be wrong. One might also describe her as a tomboy, but that would be wrong too. She didn't fit into any molds. She was exuberant about the little pleasures of life, but not consumed with looks and other fleeting things like so many of her peers.

When Hannelore was born, her mother left not long

after. Nobody ever knew where she went. The only thing left was a note saying this sort of life wasn't for her.

And maybe that's why Hannelore was so unusual, because she knew as Micah did that life wasn't fair and maybe it was better not to be too worried about things that didn't matter.

Micah was sullen by contrast and, in a way, the two needed each other. They both had trouble making friends as all the normal people didn't understand how being so different from everyone else was so natural. The pair roamed around their neighborhood every day with Jimmy, the mutt, always following along.

And goofy little Jimmy made things that much more bearable.

In Micah's mind, he and the dog had something in common. They were both treated harshly by the world, abandoned in their own unique way. That and Micah felt a little safer in a strange bed with a good mutt by his side.

Garden City was a nice home for them. It was large, but had lots of friendly people. The city was ancient, but modern in other ways. There were a few skyscrapers, but most of the homes and buildings were only two of three stories tall. The streets were busy, but many people rode bicycles wherever they went. A large river, called the Socrates, flowed through the city and fed thousands of trees and flowering bushes. Thus, the city was well named after the seemingly never-ending garden that surrounded it.

At night, the lights over the city weren't too bright and so one could see a handful of stars. This was unusual for a large city as so many places are so well lit up that the heavens have a tough time shining through.

Micah didn't notice all that as much as others, however. Looking at the stars wasn't something he did any longer.

Hannelore was a different story. "Do you think we're alone in the universe?" she said to Micah one night as the sun set and the 'evening star' which is actually the planet Venus peaked high above the park where they finished most days together.

"I don't think I care anymore," Micah said. "I used to think about things like that, but I just don't see that it matters anymore."

"Well, why would you say that?" Hannelore offered a side-eye.

"We're stuck on Earth and can't travel to the stars. We can't see what or who might be there. So does it really matter?" Micah dipped his head, disappointed in his own outlook.

"Do you want to believe that?" Hannelore frowned.

Micah looked over at her. "Doesn't matter what I want."

Hannelore stiffened her shoulders and stood up. "Well, it's getting late and dad is going to worry."

"Yeah, I guess we better go," replied Micah.

Just then a small rock came flying in and hit Micah in between the shoulders. "What's the hurry losers?"

"Oh no, it's Travis. Haven't seen him in forever." Hannelore clammed up.

Micah stood up and now with a sore spot on his back. "What do you want?"

"I'm here to get even you little jerk. You cost me an entire Summer in alternative school! I should have been hanging out with my friends, but no and it's your fault." Travis walked over to Micah and shoved him down.

Micah hit the grown with a thud.

"Leave him alone!" Hannelore teared up.

Travis was a good eleven inches taller than Micah anyway as he was unusually large for his age and had already been held back a year due to poor performance at that. Now, he towered over Micah as he lay on the ground.

"Here I thought this would be a good day," Micah said.

Travis wore a baseball cap, and he flipped it backwards. "Now you'll get the beating you deserve. No teachers to step in. No principal. No mommy or daddy to come to the rescue."

"Travis! Back off!" Hannelore stepped in between Micah and Travis.

Travis huffed. "Hannelore, you're so trashy! And if you don't get out of my way, then I'm gonna give you a beating too."

Micah's eyes sharpened. He leapt to his feet and jumped in front of Hannelore. He put up his fists with about as much grace as a newborn puppy. A professional fighter Micah was not. "I'm not afraid of you."

"You should be!" Travis reared back to take a swing.

"Excuse me young man, is there a problem here?" A deep voice came from behind.

The children turned around to see a police officer approaching. None of them said a word.

The officer walked over and stood in front of Travis. "Young man, as far as I can tell, you were about to beat these other kids up. Is that correct?"

"Um...no sir," replied Travis with a half open mouth.

The officer folded his arms. "That's not what I saw. Kid, I'll give you a warning. You better leave these other kids alone. I don't want to be the one to bring you home to your parents. And take my advice, you better straighten up or you'll have a lot bigger problems in life than a Summer in alternative school. Do I make myself clear?"

"Um...yes sir," replied Travis.

"Go on now." The officer pointed towards the nearby neighborhood.

Travis wasn't in the habit of tucking tail, but that's exactly what he did. He walked away and never looked back.

The officer turned his attention to the Micah and Hannelore. "Kids, you shouldn't be out this late. You better go on home."

"Yes sir, thank you." Hannelore smiled.

Micah trembled despite his claim of not being afraid. It took him a few seconds to appreciate that Travis wasn't coming back.

"Oh and son, we're not alone," the officer winked.

"Huh, wait...what?" Micah relaxed his fists.

The officer chuckled. "You kids were talking about being alone in the universe. I mean, you were probably talking about aliens or something silly like that, but I want you to keep something in mind." His tone softened, "none of us are ever truly alone."

The children looked at each other with blank stares.

The officer turned to walk away. "There's always someone looking out for us even when we don't know it."

The sun was down by now.

"We really better go," said Hannelore.

Just then, Jimmy the mutt strolled up.

"Where have you been? We could have used a vicious attack dog!" Micah grinned.

"I think Jimmy would have been more likely to steal Travis' hat than protect us," Hannelore giggled.

Micah turned to survey the park one last time. "Hey, where did the policeman go? He couldn't have gone far and I don't see him anymore."

"Doesn't matter Micah. We really, really need to go

before my dad grounds me," Hannelore tugged on Micah's shirt.

"Sure thing," replied Micah.

The trio took off for their street.

As Micah was about to enter his house with Jimmy in tow, Hannelore stopped him.

"Kind of lucky that policeman showed up when he did," she said.

Micah scratched his hair. "Yeah, I didn't feel like taking another pummeling."

"But ya know...it's what he said...that we're never alone." Hannelore bit her lip. "You were there for me again when Travis said he might beat me up."

"That's what friends do," Micah said.

Hannelore smiled. "Goodnight."

"See you tomorrow," he replied.

Tomorrow came, and the children spent the day with each other once again. It was the same for the day after that and the day after that.

Another school year arrived and life had settled down. The worst seemed to be behind Micah and there was no reason for him to think life would be anything other than wonderful from now on.

You see, Garden City was a safe place and any thought of danger was far off.

That was until one bright, sunny afternoon in October. A sound like thunder clamored in the skies above, but there was no storm. Nothing but a few innocent looking clouds in the sky, but the sound persisted. The roar soon turned into a rumble. Windows were rattling all over Garden City. Objects shook on the shelves of homes and shops.

Over the skies of the city, an enormous spaceship appeared. It was black as night with a few lit windows scattered across its hull. The edges were rounded, much like a blimp, but this ship was wider. There were three huge pipe shaped objects protruding from the body of the ship; one on the front, another on the back, and the third on one side. It was larger, however, and had an open hole facing outward.

The ship was the length of eleven large stadiums lined up one after the other. It was as wide as the tallest skyscraper and consumed the entire sky like no other flying object ever seen before in the long history of humankind.

It descended to a point just above the city's highest building. There it hovered. The thunder-like sound eased away, but there was still a boisterous racket heard all over the city...echoes of the rattling windows mixed with honking horns and the screams of the people below.

After a few moments, many small objects came flying out of the opening on the side of the craft. There were millions. They were spherical, about the size of a beach ball, and glowed yellow. Some took a position over the city while many more flew to locales all over the globe and within a matter of seconds they surrounded all of planet Earth.

Then came a voice emanating from each of the orbs.

A deep, grizzly voice echoed across the entire world. "My name is Vinitor, the supreme being of this galaxy. You will follow my commands or your world will suffer the consequences."

At that moment, a gigantic, planet-sized shield deployed from an even larger ship that had taken up a place in orbit. The shield unfurled like a flag and moved into place between Earth and the Sun. The shield was a dark gray color, but one would be hard pressed to see that in the darkness of space. It was thin, not unlike a piece of cloth. Made of a metal that humans had yet to discover, it was as opaque as the Moon. It blocked all sunlight from reaching the surface. The planet grew dark and much colder than usual.

Vinitor spoke again, "There's a fugitive on your planet named Taurean. He's being harbored among your people. He must be returned immediately or your planet will be denied sunlight until you all freeze to death. Bring this fugitive to my ship in this Garden City of North America. Be wise."

* * *

Back at Micah's home, he and his mother held each other after hearing the proclamation.

Elizabeth tried to hide her tears. "It will be okay, son. Somehow, some way, God will take care of us," she whispered.

Jimmy, however, acted strangely. He was pacing from one side of the house to the other. He darted out the door and ran down the street.

Micah, having grown attached to the dog, ran after him, calling out, "Jimmy, Jimmy! It's not safe! Don't go!"

But the little mutt didn't look back. He kept running.

"Micah, leave him be. Stay here!" yelled Micah's mother.

"I can't leave him out there, Mom. I'll be right back." Micah turned away from his mother and hopped on his bike. He followed Jimmy down the street.

Hannelore, who had been staring out the window at the massive ship above, noticed what was happening as Micah and the dog ran past her house. She yelled at him, "Micah, what are you doing? Come back!"

"I can't let Jimmy be out on his own. Something could

happen to him. I need that dog!" Micah yelled back at Hannelore as he was riding.

"Fine, then I'm coming with you. Stupid boy!" Hannelore shouted as she hopped on her bike and took off after them both.

The dog took them on a roundabout tour of the city. He ran across yards, parks, and down the not-so busy streets.

Micah and Hannelore followed every step of the way.

The sounds of sirens and people shouting filled the air. There were crowds of people gathered across all corners of the city shouting at police officers, who were out in force trying to calm people down. Streetlights were going haywire, blinking randomly and out of sync with each other.

Micah heard a whirling, buzzing noise over his head. He looked up to notice that, not too far above the rooftops, these glowing yellow orbs flew about like a swarm of bees minding their hive.

Each orb emitted a bright white light that was rapidly moving back and forth over the buildings and shining through the windows. These little devices were scanning every inch of the city. They were looking for something.

Jimmy paid no attention to any of it. He ran with a purpose as though he had somewhere to be, but where would a dog need to be at a time like this?

Micah then noticed that the little mutt was leading them directly under the spaceship. "Jimmy! Come back!"

Not only was the ship massive, but to look at it from below was like looking at another world. This other world, that had come down to make a visit upon the Earth, was the most frightening thing Micah had ever seen.

On the bottom of the ship, he could see hundreds of pulsating circles. They were engines keeping the ship afloat, but made no noise. He was so taken aback by it all he nearly crashed his bike into a parked car.

In Micah's mind, his job was to protect his newfound friend from the indescribable danger that awaited anyone who approached this ship. So he tried to stay focused on Jimmy.

This troublesome dog ran into a large park under the tip of the ship. After racing through block after block of the city, he came to a rest.

Micah and Hannelore whipped in behind Jimmy.

The little mutt turned around to look at the two children and then his appearance changed. He grew taller and wider as if by magic. His fur changed into pasty gray skin, his dark brown eyes into big blue circles. His snout transformed into a big red nose stretching from the base of his eyes to the top of his mouth. Instead of four legs, he now had two arms and just two legs. If that wasn't shocking enough, he then spoke, "I'm sorry Micah. I've lied to you. My name is Taurean. I'm the one they want and for the sake of this world, I have to turn myself in. You need to go home now. I promise you and your people will be safe after they've taken me."

Micah fell off his bike and Hannelore pinched herself to make sure she wasn't dreaming.

"Go now, hurry! They'll take me soon," said Taurean.

"What are you?" asked Micah.

"I'm your friend, young one. Never forget that. But for now, I must go. I'm sorry to have caused you any trouble. Please go before they become suspicious of you," Taurean said. He then looked up at the ship with sullen eyes as if he faced nothing short of mortal danger.

At that moment, a bright light several yards in diameter shone down from the ship above. It was a tractor beam.

Taurean, Micah, Hannelore, and even their bikes levitated off the ground and brought nearer to the ship.

"I'm sorry, children. This is my fault. I should have told you sooner," Taurean spoke as he buried his face in his hands.

Hannelore screamed, but they could do nothing.

Micah didn't know what to do. He thought of his father and wondered if he too would meet a tragic end in the sky.

The voice of Vinitor echoed through the night once again as he greeted his new captives. "Taurean, enemy of mine and your Earthling accomplices, I thought surely you would make this planet wait until the brink of death. I appreciate your quickness in obeying my command. You'll make fine slaves." Vinitor laughed.

The ship swallowed them and the opening closed behind them.

CHAPTER 2

ARMED, helmeted, and black-uniformed guards escorted Micah, Hannelore, and Taurean down a long hallway on the ship to a room with a high ceiling and a large chair placed in the center.

On the chair sat Vinitor, a miserable creature. He wore a black helmet with a glowing yellow triangle on its face mask that hid his eyes. His drooling mouth was there for all to see, however. He had four arms and three legs. Dressed in black armor and standing about eight feet tall, he was quite an imposing figure.

Vinitor stood up and waved his scepter. "Taurean, where's the Convergence? You must have hidden it on this world. Tell me where it is or I'll destroy this planet."

Taurean approached the creature and begged him not to harm the people of Earth. "Your quarrel is with me, Master Vinitor. There's no need for this planet to suffer."

"There's a need as long as I say there's a need. Tell me where the Convergence is and this will all end." Vinitor struck the floor with his scepter.

Micah and Hannelore barely stood straight, their knees

and ankles weak. They looked at each other intently, held hands, and turned once again toward Vinitor and Taurean.

"Master Vinitor, I'll give you the Convergence if you spare this planet. These people don't even know it exists. They had no part in my escape or my hiding here, least of all these two children." Taurean pointed toward Micah and Hannelore.

"Ah yes, what are these two puny humans if not co-conspirators?" The villain pointed the scepter at the children. "I should disintegrate them right now to prove just how serious I am."

Micah and Hannelore ducked down to the floor when Vinitor pointed at them.

Suddenly, there came the sound of an explosion in the distance. Then came another and another. The ship shook and its otherworldly metal creaked and bent.

Vinitor's eyes glanced upwards, if one could have seen them behind his helmet that is. "What is that?"

Outside Vinitor's ship, a small craft had descended upon the mammoth invader in the sky. It was a bright white color, similar to the shape of a wishbone. It fired repeatedly upon Vinitor's ship and by now was targeted by the exterior gunners.

The small craft made a second pass on Vinitor's ship and this time dropped a bomb just over the throne room where Vinitor himself stood.

A bright fiery flash later, bits of metal and wire flew away from the ceiling. The darkened sky peered through on the other side of a newly formed hole.

"A Warden is here! Summon my best guards!" The creature moaned into a microphone attached to one of his wrists.

Micah, Hannelore, and Taurean were all stunned. They

froze right where they were and awaited whatever chaos was surely to ensue.

The small craft took another pass at Vinitor's ship and flew once again right over the hole created a moment earlier. A figure jumped out of the cabin of the ship and fell directly into the opening. The ship itself kept flying and was now being followed by ten fighters that had deployed from the mammoth invader.

The figure who had jumped out of the ship slowed his descent with thrusters attached to his feet and elbows. He landed in the middle of the room, stooped down, and fired a stun weapon at the guards overseeing Micah and Hannelore.

The guards dropped like sacks of potatoes.

"What is your name Warden? So I may put it on your tombstone!" Vinitor shouted.

The figure turned around and looked at Vinitor. "My name is Darbian and I've survived far worse creatures than you." Darbian was human looking and wore a white suit with armor over much of his body. Tall and muscular, he stood down a villain such as Vinitor as though it were his third or fourth so far this day.

Just then, Darbian took out a small, round metal object from his belt. He tossed it toward the wall and it exploded, creating a large hole in the side of spacecraft. "Come along children, and you too Mr. Armankouri. It's time to vacate the premises."

Micah and Hannelore raced toward Darbian and asked him what they were to do.

"We're going to jump. My ship will catch us. No time to question the wisdom of this; it's now or never."

Micah and Hannelore questioned the wisdom nonetheless, but they had seen so many strange things today. The thought of jumping off the edge of the ship seemed not so odd compared to the other things they had just experienced. The four of them ran for the opening.

Two dozen guards flooded the throne room just as the four ran. They leapt out of the ship and were instantly teleported aboard Darbian's ship which, at that moment, was making a pass over the opening as it head straight down toward the ground.

The craft weaved in and around the city's skyscrapers. Dipping and bobbing yet moving through the air as smoothly as a bird.

Vinitor's fighters were in hot pursuit and closing fast. Every few seconds they fired their laser weapons at Darbian's ship, sometimes hitting but mostly missing.

Aboard Darbian's ship, everything seemed rather calm. And it should be noted that this was no mere spacecraft. It possessed some of the most advanced technology in the universe including an internal gravity field that kept Darbian and all of his new passengers comfortable and upright while the craft made hairpin turns around buildings and sudden shifts upwards and downwards.

"Gregorical, how many fighters are following us?" Darbian spoke into thin air.

"Ten, sir. Do you wish for us to fire back?" responded Gregorical in a muffled but human sounding voice.

"Let me get to the bridge first," Darbian replied.

"Who's that?" Micah asked as he spun around looking for the source of the voice.

"That's Gregorical, the ship. He has a mind of his own you might say." Darbian chuckled. "Don't you have artificial intelligence on your planet?"

"Not that I know of," Hannelore chimed.

"How did we get into the ship? I don't remember." Micah asked as he walked closer to their newfound friend.

"We teleported. Don't tell me you don't have that on your planet either." Darbian's paced quickened.

Hannelore touched the shiny white walls of the interior as the group walked down a broad corridor. "This thing is amazing."

"I'm pleased that you like my walls. We haven't properly made our acquaintance, however," the voice of Gregorical shot through the air.

"My name is Hannelore. This is my best friend, Micah. And this is his dog Jimmy," Hannelore pointed toward Taurean.

Darbian looked at Taurean. "I suppose you've been shape shifting, Mr. Armankouri, and I imagine a proper introduction is in order."

"Quite right, sir. My name is Taurean of Armankour. I must insist, however, that we delay our pleasantries. Vinitor has not come looking for me but for an object in my possession. We must retrieve it immediately. Vinitor can never possess it. Can you help us?" Taurean put his hands together almost as though he were begging, but begging wasn't the custom of the Armankouri people. They put their hands together to make polite requests.

"Consider us at your service, Taurean. Gregorical and I will do everything in our power to help you retrieve it," Darbian replied.

Just then, they arrived at the bridge of the ship. There was a large round screen at the front showing where the craft was going. The children didn't realize the craft was flying evasively. Stunned at the views from above their home of Garden City, they were hooked on the screen as though it had captured them. Even more stunned at how quickly the scenery changed from one second to another, they gasped and awed.

"I think I'm going to be airsick," said Micah.

Darbian stooped to get eye level with Micah. "Don't look at the screen, young one. Focus on the back of the room instead. We'll be out of this mess soon enough." Darbian stood back up and went to the front of the bridge.

Micah and Hannelore turned instead to the back of the room where they saw blinking lights and machines of all kinds along the walls. There was a station at the center of the room with multiple screens and buttons and levers all around it. It was circular with four seats around it.

It tickled Micah's imagination. All the years he had dreamed of being an astronaut and now he was in a spaceship surrounded by gadgets and inventions beyond human understanding.

Taurean tapped Darbian on the elbow. "Master Darbian, we must reach the Palace Hotel in the center of the city. That's where I've hidden the Convergence and we must retrieve it before Vinitor's soldiers find it."

The lights blinked aboard the ship.

"They're landing more hits Gregorical. Time to fly for real," Darbian shouted.

The fighters outside had split into three groups and were chasing Gregorical from multiple angles.

"There sir, the river will lead you to the hotel," Taurean pointed at the display.

Darbian commanded Gregorical to fly along the surface of the river. Meanwhile, Darbian sat in his captain's chair directing laser fire at the fighters.

Gregorical was quite nimble. He plummeted himself toward the river and pulled up at the last possible instant.

Two fighters crashed into the river as they could not match Gregorical's expert movements.

Gregorical sustained several more hits, however; and with the first shift anyone had experienced on this flight, a quarter of the left section of the ship ruptured and came flying off. With navigation now limited, Gregorical flew as upright as he could and landed on the street in front of the hotel. The ship skid along the street and smashed through a large water fountain right in front of the building. There, Gregorical came to rest.

Sparks flew out all sides of the ship. Now sitting beside the grand and luxurious hotel, one could see that Gregorical was about three stories high and fifty yards long.

Inside, Darbian and his passengers were fine, but frazzled with their predicament.

As Gregorical sat with a piece of his left stern broken off, he spoke, "Darbian, now would be a good time to hurry. It will take me several minutes to repair myself and the lack of solar energy will make it even more difficult. At that, my teleportation device is damaged."

"Taurean, take me inside to your device. We must work quickly. Children, you stay here. You'll be safe with Gregorical." Darbian walked back through the corridor from which they came only moments ago.

Taurean followed, and the two leaped out of the gaping hole left by the ripped apart stern of Gregorical. They found themselves on the sidewalk.

There were hundreds of people mulling around outside. Some of them were flooding out of the hotel as they feared the craft would hit the building. Others came out of neighboring buildings. Frightened and confused, they rushed to call loved ones. Unfortunately, their concerns were about to grow more dire.

At that moment, several of the fighters that had been in pursuit arrived at the scene. They surrounded Gregorical and all the people on the street including Darbian and Taurean. There the fighters hovered with their guns trained.

CHAPTER 3

"MASTER DARBIAN, what do we do now?" Taurean asked as he peered toward a sky filled with fighters.

Darbian looked at the hovering craft. Then he turned to Taurean. "They're drones. Their command was to follow the ship. If we slip into the hotel, they shouldn't notice us. Getting back to Gregorical and the children, that will be the problem," Darbian said as he walked toward the entrance to the hotel.

Taurean followed and the two jogged into the lobby of the building.

"Master Darbian, we should take the stairs. The Convergence is hidden on the fifth floor."

As the two raced up the stairs, Taurean told his story of coming to Earth.

"I came to this world to hide the Convergence. Never in a millennium would I have thought someone would be able to find me. I left no trace of myself. I used the Convergence to travel into the future. How is it possible for someone to find you in the future when you've disappeared into thin air?" Taurean threw his hands up in the air in frustration.

"You did what?" Darbian stopped. He stooped down to Taurean's eye level. "You traveled here from the past using this device?"

Taurean frowned. "Yes. It was of the utmost importance that the Convergence never be discovered. I thought the best course of action was to travel to the most remote planet I could think of and then proceed into a future time. If one were to travel into the past, then one would leave evidence of one's presence. There would be a trail to follow. I couldn't risk that. If I were to travel to the future, however, then no one would know where to look. I don't understand how anyone found me. I told no one where I was going! When I arrived, I made sure to destroy my ship. I planned to live the rest of my life here among the humans. That's when I met Micah, so lonely and wounded. I felt for him, but now I've put him and Hannelore in mortal danger. How did anyone find me? I don't understand!"

"It takes a time traveler to find a time traveler," said Darbian. "Come now, we need to retrieve this device of yours." Darbian pointed to the top of the stair well.

The two climbed the steps once again until they reached the fifth floor. When they came out of the stairwell, they found several people huddled in the hallway.

A few of them shouted as they assumed Taurean was one of the invaders.

"Keep calm everyone; we're the good guys," shouted Darbian as he whirled around to look at people on all sides of him.

"This way, Master Darbian, I've hidden the device under the bed I first slept in here." Taurean jumped up and down as they approached the room...5 1 2.

The two barged into the room. They found no one in the room and that was fortunate as neither thought ahead and concerned himself with having to explain their presence to a half dressed guest.

"You hid the device under the furniture?" Darbian marveled.

"Absolutely," Taurean remarked. "Everyone on this planet knows they don't clean under the beds in hotels. It's a rather dirty world, actually."

Darbian flipped on the light switch.

Taurean crawled under the bed and retrieved a small silver canister about the size of a basketball. He was very dusty when he emerged from under the bed, but that was the least of his worries.

"Master Darbian, we have to get the Convergence off this planet and away from Vinitor at all costs. I'm almost positive of who he's working for and if the Halinkoy Cult ever obtains the Convergence then life as we know it would be in danger." Taurean rubbed his brow and then set the device on a table in the middle of the room.

"The Halinkoy Cult? Why have I never heard of them?" Darbian responded as he rubbed his chin.

"I'm not sure, Master Darbian, but be mindful...the Halinkoy Cult is the ancient enemy of the Armankouri people. I came here to hide the Convergence from them, hoping against hope they could never use it against us." Taurean sat down and punched buttons on a small key pad on the side of the Convergence.

"I've heard of the Relic Destroyers, the Dragonfly People, and others certainly, but I've never heard of the Halinkoy Cult. Taurean, you know more about what's going on here than you're letting on. You said you traveled through time using this? What exactly is the Convergence?

It's more than a time machine. What makes it so dangerous?" Darbian sat down at the table besides Taurean.

"The Convergence was created by my people many generations ago. It was used to transport an entire planet and an entire people through time and space. We used it to avoid slaughter at the hands of our enemies. There were always some among my people who wanted us to abandon our pacifist ways and develop weapons. Instead, our scientists created the Convergence. We used it many times and always successfully. Then something terrible happened." Taurean paused and looked at Darbian right in the eyes. "One of our people betrayed us...one of our top scientists who helped build the Convergence. He took the device and sold it to the highest bidder. Oh, Master Darbian, this happened thousands of years ago and we can't do anything about it now, but the one who bought the device was a human named Ajax Halinkoy. It's the reason I came to this planet and not any of the others. I thought if the Halinkoy Cult was searching for the Convergence then the last place they would go is to Ajax' own planet. Nothing terribly important has ever happened here and the technology isn't at all advanced. Halinkoy left this planet behind a long time ago. Who would have thought he might look back?"

"A human with the power to move through time and space? There must be more to the story," Darbian quipped.

"Not a great deal is known about Halinkoy. He comes and goes and he destroys. That seems to be his only aim." Taurean squinted one of his eyes and examined the device more closely.

Darbian leaned back in his chair. "Well, how did you get the Convergence back? You never involved the Wardein? Why not?"

"We don't know what Halinkoy used the Convergence

for. We don't know if he used it at all. And we didn't have to involve the Wardein. Some time ago a Warden of mythical proportions, of whom we don't even have a name, stole the Convergence from Halinkoy and returned it to our people. Ever since then, we've been hiding it. We can't even risk keeping it on our planet anymore. We've had to devise new ways to avoid our enemies. Allowing the Convergence to fall into the wrong hands would be disastrous. It would cost countless innocent lives and my people cannot allow that to happen." Taurean went back to work on the Convergence.

Darbian cocked his head to the side. "Ok, explain something. The Convergence is needed on Armankour to move the planet when it's threatened. You brought it here to hide it from Halinkoy, but you never intended on going back? That doesn't make any sense."

Taurean relaxed. "Yes, it's quite complicated. I should tell you I took the Convergence without permission from the Council."

"You did what?" Darbian jumped from his chair and threw his hands up.

"I'm a bit too much like my father, I'm afraid. I act when action is necessary." Taurean went back to punching buttons.

Darbian pointed back at Taurean. "How is it you get to decide when action is necessary? You've put the people of Earth in danger and you didn't even have your Council's blessing to come here?"

Taurean stared straight ahead. "It was in the best interest of my people, I assure you."

Darbian whipped back around. "How so?"

"We were attacked. As I told you, Halinkoy destroys. Over the centuries, he attacked us many times. He always failed. That was until his most recent attempt." Taurean sniffled.

"What are you getting at?" Darbian said.

"Armankour has fallen. Our people have been scattered. We're being hunted to extinction. Perhaps the faction that wanted us to create weapons was right all along. I'm not sure." Taurean wiped his eyes. "It doesn't matter now."

Darbian froze in his tracks. "How is that possible?"

"Honestly, we don't know how it happened. Halinkoy used some weapon to cause our Reality Shields to work against us. A Reality Shield works by deflecting energy weapons harmlessly into another dimension. Generally, they work perfectly," Taurean said.

"But?" Darbian replied.

"Whatever Halinkoy hit us with caused the Reality Shield to work in reverse. Suddenly, the alternate dimensions were flooding the planet and causing untold destruction. Our only option was to shut the Shields down and flee. It was chaos. There was little time to prepare. My office was responsible for keeping track of the Convergence so I took it and left the planet. Others left and took our technologies with them hoping to protect them from Halinkoy." Taurean turned his face up to Darbian. "Armankour doesn't really exist anymore. The Ruling Council doesn't really exist anymore. We're stretched across the corners of the universe...on our own so to speak."

"I don't understand. The Wardein would have helped. Why did you allow yourself to be attacked repeatedly?" Darbian sat down next to Taurean.

"It's a mystery to us, but the Warden that recovered the Convergence so many generations ago told us never to involve the Wardein with the Halinkoy Cult. The only explanation that solider offered us was this...'the future depends on it.' We didn't know what to make of it except that perhaps the space-time continuum had been thrown out of whack." Taurean covered his eyes with his hands. "We've made great sacrifices Darbian, but I don't have any idea why."

Darbian shook his head. "Something is terribly wrong here."

"The only explanation is that time travelers have been at work and doing a dastardly work at that. We may never comprehend what has happened, but please understand that this device must be hidden at all costs. Do you understand, Master Darbian? All costs." Taurean looked down and fiddled with his fingers. "I know now what we must do. We can't destroy the Convergence because it would cause a rift in the space-time continuum. We must, however, hide it where no one can find it."

"How do we do that?" Darbian's tone grew dire.

"The last few minutes, I've been adjusting the controls. Normally, a person must input a time and place and then accompany the device to its destination, but what if we set the device to travel on its own to a time and place even we don't know?" Taurean cracked a sly smile.

"You're thinking if no one knows when or where the device ends up then no one could track it? That it would be lost to all of civilization forevermore?" Darbian stood up and turned his back, looking out the window onto the street below.

"Yes, that's it. It's the only way to secure the future. The Convergence will choose where to hide and no one can follow it." Taurean further adjusted the controls.

"But how would we be sure that no one could track it? We don't know how Vinitor found it here. He knew you were here with it and that's another mystery. There are too many unknowns, Taurean. The first thing to do is take it to the Wardein Central Command. The Conference of Wardein can devise a plan to hide it safely away from any threat." Darbian spoke this but wasn't terribly confident in his own words. He perceived there was so much more going on than what he could understand. He knew that implicitly trusting the Conference of Wardein to handle the situation, as he would normally do, might not be possible.

"We don't have much time to think about it, Master Darbian. Vinitor and his guards will be here soon enough, as they surely know by now that Gregorical has been damaged and is sitting in the street. We might not even get away from Vinitor. How could we get back to the Wardein Central Command?" Taurean's eyes sunk.

"Don't you worry about Gregorical. There are plenty of tricks up his sleeve. And he's got more fight in him than any army Vinitor can muster." Darbian put his hands on the window. "But you're right about one thing; Vinitor and his guards are here! We have to get back to Gregorical and the children!"

"I'm right behind you, Master Darbian." Taurean picked up the Convergence.

The two rushed out of the door and back down the stairs.

Meanwhile, Vinitor and a battalion of his guards arrived on the scene. They stood on top of a group of craft that hovered a few stories above the street.

Vinitor stretched all four of his arms out. "People of Earth, aliens alike, and especially you Warden, bow before the supreme being of the galaxy!"

Darbian and Taurean came out of the hotel at that moment.

"Supreme being of the galaxy? Vinitor, you're nothing

but a glorified bounty hunter! Who are you working for?" Darbian shouted from the street below.

"Ahhh, you insult me, you pitiful Warden. Your ship is battered. You're surrounded. You're defeated," Vinitor answered. His voice then grew more subdued. "And it's no business of yours who I'm working for."

Darbian and Taurean inched toward the ship. The people around them were huddled together and bowing down.

Vinitor peered down at Taurean. "I see you've finally brought the Convergence. Good boy. Now hand it here before I freeze this planet anyway!"

Taurean set the Convergence down and moved away from it.

The device made quite a bit of noise, a thunderous sound. It spun and a bright light emanated from the core of the device. The outer shell became transparent and the light within shined through. A high-pitched sound filled the air and the light grew so bright that everyone within sight of the device had to cover their eyes. Then it disappeared. A glowing portion of pavement was all that was left behind.

CHAPTER 4

INSIDE THE SHIP, the children stared at the screen as images of the drones transmitted in.

"How are we going to get out of this?" Hannelore asked as she gripped the arms of her chair. Her knuckles were white and her fingernails dug into the cushioning.

"Gregorical said he could heal himself. We should be able to take off again soon and outrun these blasted things." Micah bit his upper lip.

"Are you trying to reassure me or yourself?" Hannelore asked.

"Both," replied Micah.

Gregorical spoke. "I'm attempting to reboot my growth protocol and heal my stern. It's taking quite some time. Usually, I can absorb solar energy from the surrounding environment. Unfortunately, Vinitor has blocked direct sunlight from entering the planet's atmosphere. Children, are you aware of any alternative source of energy on this planet?"

Micah sat up straight with wide eyes. He had never been addressed by a spaceship before.

"He's talking to you, Micah. You went to the Star Force Academy," Hannelore quipped.

"I didn't go to the Academy. I went through the Junior Program." Micah got up and paced around his chair.

Hannelore tapped the panel in front of her. "Well, what did they teach you?"

Micah walked forward and looked at the main screen. Sweat dripped down his forehead. He never expected to encounter such danger when he woke up this morning, but the moment had his brain churning for ideas. "Gregorical, can you absorb ambient energy?"

"Yes, I believe that would work. You're a sharp one," Gregorical said.

"What's ambient energy?" Hannelore got up and stood next to Micah in front of the screen.

"It's all the unused and wasted energy floating around in the atmosphere. They have plans to use it to power cars and such, but nobody's gotten around to it." Micah shrugged his shoulders.

"Recalibrating now and yes, it appears there is ample ambient energy within range. It should take just a few minutes to heal myself." Gregorical changed the display on the main screen to show that the leftmost wing of his stern was now growing like a plant.

Before their eyes, large pieces of metal grafted together with small ones. All the rough edges evened out. A new engine and even an exhaust port developed at the end of the marvelous machine. Both the right and left sections of the stern glowed just as they had when the craft was in flight. The ship was ready to take off once again.

* * *

Outside the ship, Darbian and Taurean had just witnessed the Convergence disappearing.

"Taurean, what did you do? That was a mistake, a huge mistake," Darbian said as he put his hands over the top of his temples.

"It had to be done, Master Darbian. No one can find it now." Taurean looked up at Vinitor and shouted. "You'll have no victory today! You'll never find the Convergence now!"

Darbian whispered to Taurean. "We don't know that for certain, Taurean, and even if we did, what about Earth? What's your plan for getting Vinitor and his shield away from this planet?"

"I didn't think that far ahead, Master Darbian." Taurean's eyes jutted back and forth between Vinitor and Darbian. "Surely, he'll leave now since he has nothing to gain. Or perhaps he won't. I'm sorry; I didn't know what else to do." Taurean sat down on the pavement.

"Now what are you doing?" Darbian grimaced.

"Perhaps I've failed again." Taurean's face turned green and everyone knows the Armankouri have green blood and that it rushes to their face when they're ashamed.

Darbian continued to whisper. "You should have allowed me to take it to the Wardein Central Command." Darbian looked up at Vinitor to gauge his reaction.

The self-proclaimed supreme being stepped forward and looked down upon where the Convergence had sat. "What did you mongrels do with it?" A great deal of saliva fell from his mouth as he shouted. He let out a bellow as though he were in pain and thrust his staff against the floor of the craft he was standing upon. "I'll make you pay for this!"

Just then, Darbian noticed that Gregorical had finished

healing his stern portion. He looked back to Vinitor. "If you want to find the Convergence, then you'll have to chase us!" He paused, put his wrist up to his mouth, and spoke into it. "Gregorical, we're ready to come aboard."

"Of course," Gregorical's voice echoed back.

The two teleported aboard Gregorical once again.

Vinitor ordered the drones to fire on the Warden's ship for a second time.

Quick and keen laser shots came from all directions around the ship. Blast after blast created sparks all across the ship's hull, but nothing penetrated.

The people outside the hotel screamed. They ran in every direction away from the fighting.

Darbian spoke, "Gregorical, I've got an idea on how to get out of here. Take off, loop backwards right into the midst of those soldiers."

"Yes, sir," answered Gregorical.

The thrusters fired. He took off, flew forwards for an instant, looped up in the air, and came down into the middle of Vinitor and his soldiers.

The soldiers were firing as well although one would think they were aiming for the windows on nearby buildings.

The fire of the drones followed the ship and caught the battallion in their crossfire.

"No, no, you stupid machines! Cease fire, cease fire!" Vinitor ducked down, waved his hands frantically, and shouted at the drones.

Some of Vinitor's soldiers fell dead, victims of drone fire.

Gregorical took advantage of the confusion to fly straight upwards and away from the discombobulated mass of drones and soldiers.

"That ought to leave them in a bind for a while," Darbian smiled.

"The Warden is getting away and with him goes the knowledge of the Convergence. Drones, follow him! Follow that ship!" Vinitor ripped off his helmet to reveal a creature with three eyes. All of them bloodshot, they each chose a different direction; each falling upon various cowering groups of humans.

The rest of the drones flew up like arrows into the atmosphere and followed Gregorical.

Darbian looked at Micah and Hannelore. "Children, I'm afraid I will have to take you with me. Vinitor will think you know where to find the Convergence. He'll take you captive again if I don't protect you. I'm sorry, but you can't go home right now," Darbian said as he flipped a few switches on the main control panel.

"That sounds like a fantastic idea," Micah responded.

"It does?" Darbian asked.

"I've wanted nothing more than to fly through space," Micah's eyes transfixed on the images from the main screen that showed the sky growing black and the moon approaching.

"I guess that's a good thing," said Darbian.

Hannelore didn't exude enthusiasm. Her fingernails had tiny bits of cushioning under them. There were still chill bumps running up and down her arms. "What about the shield that's blocking the sunlight?" She managed.

"Good question my girl. Gregorical, what do you propose we do about that shield? We can't leave the planet without doing away with it. I'm sure that Vinitor would hold such a threat in place to make sure we would succumb to his demands." Darbian's pupils widened as the adrenaline flowed.

"Sir, our lasers aren't strong enough to do significant damage," Gregorical responded.

Darbian swallowed a little saliva. "I didn't think so, but maybe we could trick a few of those drones into helping us out, eh?"

Gregorical switched the display to an image of Vinitor's command ship flying away from the Earth and towards their position. "Sir, he's following us."

"I wonder what type of weapons that thing has?" Darbian activated a sensor array to examine the command ship.

Taurean piped up. "Why not draw Vinitor in? Force him to ram his own device!"

Darbian whipped around. "That's brilliant Taurean! Gregorical, can you get them to chase us at high speed?"

"I'll do my best sir," Gregorical responded.

Vinitor's fighters were little match for Gregorical's evasiveness in the open environment of space. Their laser fire rarely struck their target. Now, the command ship itself would fall prey to the superior flying machine.

Gregorical flew straight toward the shield on a collision course, in fact.

Vinitor's command ship followed and fired large balls of energy that when exploded would ignite the gases around their intended target. These as well failed to hit Gregorical.

"Full speed ahead pilot!" Vinitor was furious that he had yet to damage the wishbone shaped ship.

"Sir, we're heading for the shield. If we continue at our current pace, we won't be able to stop in time," cried the pilot aboard the command ship.

"Forget the shield, pilot. We have to catch that Warden!" Vinitor was not the best long term decision maker.

Gregorical flew ever closer to the shield and with Vinitor in hot pursuit, he pulled up at the last instant and skimmed the surface of the shield, causing a wake to flow across as though it were the surface of an ocean.

Vinitor observed this and collapsed back into his throne. "What an utter mess this Warden has made of me."

As Gregorical flew out of sight, Vinitor's command ship flew head long into the nearly planet sized shield that had been the centerpiece of his plan to capture the Convergence.

The shield cracked like glass and shattered into millions of tiny pieces.

By contrast, the command ship suffered little damage as the metal of the shield was designed to block sunlight, not spaceships.

In the confusion of the moment, Gregorical engaged his interstellar engines and flew off like a lightning bolt.

Darbian and his makeshift crew were nowhere to be seen by the invader and his henchmen.

After several moments of oscillating between angry fits and self-loathing, Vinitor relaxed for a moment and surveyed the aftermath of the battle. At that moment a ghastly idea fully percolated. "We will take the command ship back down to the surface. There we will abduct some of these humans. We might need them for collateral. That's all they're good for anyway." He motioned to his battalion to fulfill his orders.

The command ship lowered back down to Garden City and there Vinitor and his battalion exited the ship once more.

This time they trained their weapons on the bystanders below.

Large masses of people, who had all just been through a

harrowing ordeal, were ordered to march several blocks where they boarded the command ship. They hesitated at first, but complied as they feared for their lives.

Vinitor led his brigade back to the command ship and oversaw the humans being levitated inside. Hundreds of innocent people were caught in this plot. What the bounty hunter had in mind for them if he wasn't able to obtain the Convergence, not even he knew. Perhaps he would turn them to slaves. Perhaps he would sell them off to space pirates. He wasn't thinking that far ahead because, for the moment, he was consumed with finding Darbian, acquiring this Convergence, and then trading it for his bounty.

With his orders fulfilled, Vinitor boarded his ship along with the rest of his battalion.

* * *

Gregorical was far ahead by now. They sped out of the solar system as quickly as they had appeared.

"I suppose we've gotten away for now," said Darbian.

Micah and Hannelore were far more enthralled with the view of the main screen. They saw planets and moons whizzing by, the blackness of space, and a starry background of which they had only dreamed.

"Children," Darbian uttered. "I want you to go in the back. Gregorical will direct you. We may be in for a bumpy ride, and I don't want you to be preoccupied with what's happening up here."

"I can handle myself," responded Micah. "The Junior Star Force officers certainly thought so."

Hannelore glared at Micah as earlier he was unimpressed with his own qualifications.

"I've always wanted to be an astronaut. My father was

an astronaut. He taught me everything he knew. I can help you!" Micah responded as he gripped Darbian's arm.

The real reason Darbian wanted the children to go into one of the back rooms was because he wanted to make plans with Taurean on what to do next. That and he intended to give the shape shifter a good tongue-lashing for not listening earlier.

"Fine, you're an astronaut, Micah, but I'm a Warden. I'm sworn to protect those who need protecting and to help those who can't help themselves. That includes astronauts. You and Hannelore go on back. I'll be back there in a moment." Darbian spoke firmly but kindly. When he finished telling the children what to do, he looked down again at the panel he was working on.

"Gregorical knows to listen. Perhaps I'll just talk to him," Micah said as he turned around and walked away.

Hannelore followed. "Micah, don't be disappointed. You've never fought a battle with an intergalactic warlord before. Darbian knows what he's doing."

Micah stared ahead.

The two walked to the back of the craft as Gregorical directed them along the way.

"Micah," said Gregorical. "I want you to look at something. Hannelore, he'll need your help. I want you to watch a recording on the history of the Wardein. Would you two do that for me?"

Both answered yes.

"I think it will help you understand what we're up against," Gregorical responded.

* * *

Back on the bridge, Darbian received a recorded message

from Vinitor, "I have hundreds of these humans aboard my ship. I've given our encounter some thought and I have no plans to chase you very far. I've recalled my drones. What I want is for you to meet me in an hour at the Belt of Orion and give me the Convergence, or I'll punish these people. You know I will. Remember, you have one hour."

CHAPTER 5

"OH DEAR, this situation keeps getting more complicated," Taurean looked up at Darbian. There was red in his face and everyone knows Armankouri get a little red-faced when they're scared.

"We need backup. We need other Wardein to assist in the rescue. That's what I was getting at earlier. The Wardein are stronger when they're together. If we had teamed up then we overwhelming Vinitor wouldn't have been difficult." Darbian stood up and walked to the communication device.

Taurean stood up and bowed his head to the floor. "I'm sorry, Master Darbian, but I couldn't take any chances. I don't think you understand how terrible it would be if the Convergence should fall into the hands of the Halinkoy Cult."

Darbian placed his hand onto an imprint to activate the communication device. He adjusted a large, blue dial until the right frequency appeared. "This is Warden Darbian of the 401st District. Innocent people in my district are in danger

46

and I require help. I've encountered the bounty hunter Vinitor, and he has hundreds of hostages. I'm not equipped to take him on alone so I require as many Wardein as can be spared."

He waited a few moments, but there was no response.

"Why aren't they responding? This is highly unusual. We don't have time to wait for them. We need to be at the Belt of Orion in less than an hour from now." Darbian paced around with his hands on his hips.

Taurean turned around to speak. "I don't understand. Wardein are the most prompt soldiers in the universe. Where could they be?"

Darbian propped himself up on the control panel and stared over it at Taurean. "We might not be in this mess if you had listened. Getting Vinitor to destroy his own shield and leave Earth wasn't that hard. He's not a maniac; he only wants money."

Taurean pointed up. "Perhaps we give him money?"

Darbian curled his lip. "I'm a Warden, I don't carry money Taurean. The corps provides everything. Do you have money?"

"Of course not, I was just a dog this morning," responded Taurean.

"Getting Vinitor to leave the planet was easy enough, but I didn't think far enough ahead. If only I were more experienced. We have nothing to give him and it's my fault," Darbian said.

"Risk him getting the Convergence? That was never an option!" Taurean extended his hand palms down and pressed against the air.

Darbian sighed. "No, but we don't have a bargaining chip. No leverage and we've got to meet him soon. There's no reason for him to give us those people. At this point, I'm not even sure he would spare their lives. He might be so angry that he would kill them to spite us."

* * *

Meanwhile, in the back of the ship, Micah and Hannelore watched the recording given to them by Gregorical.

A narrator spoke. "Ladies, gentleman, and artificial life forms; the following is a presentation on the history of the Wardein. The universe's trained protectors thank you for your attention."

Images of black space with intermittent stars filled the screen. "Many millions of years ago, no one knows how long ago, and before the Councils of the Planets, the universe was a chaotic place. There was no rule of law. The peoples of the universe did as they pleased and often harmed each other without a second thought. Factions of pirates dominated vast portions of space and lay in wait for travelers. The Wiskolo, or Firebreathers as they are more commonly called, ravaged any and every race with which they came into contact. Brutes, they were held back only by their inability to reason and cooperate. The earliest civilizations were intelligent people, but possessed no ability to fend off great evildoers. They had no chance to beat back the greatest villains of them all, the Tammeder Clan."

The recording showed depictions of the foes of the ancient past. "The Tammeder were unlike any people who had come before or since. They were evil to the bone, kind only to one another. They lived to destroy. Their technology was advanced, and they used it to full effect. The great sin of the Tammeder was in targeting planets, capturing the innocent peoples, and forcing them into slave labor. The peoples not deemed suitable for slavery were wiped out. They grew powerful and plentiful. Over the millennia, they formed their own religion. They worshipped their king like he was a god and they came to believe anyone not loyal to the Tammeder king must be destroyed so as not to fill the universe with inferior beings as the Tammeder would say."

The presentation continued. "After many millennia of conquering, enslaving peoples, and committing genocide; they invented their greatest weapon of all...the World Killers. These weapons were used to fire large asteroid-like energy pulses at any target. Enough strikes with this weapon and an entire world would disintegrate. Each ship possessed the World Killer technology and there were millions upon millions of ships. The Tammeder would try to pound a planet into submission and if the people did not relent and give into being slaves, then destruction would follow. Many people were erased from history by the Tammeder Clan."

The children looked at each other and almost cried.

"With this growing threat, the wisest civilizations came together to devise a plan to defeat these forces of evil. This was the First Council of Planets. The Armankouri, the Caladi, the Araces, the Quinpalian, the Envaygius, the Finshalu, and the Nexarum, or the Star Chasers, met for a historic event. Together, they planned to defeat the enemies of all free peoples. They all offered their finest warriors and their most brilliant technologies and they created the Wardein, a corps of warriors dedicated to peace in the universe. As the ranks of the Wardein grew, they engaged the Tammeder ever more frequently. While there were early losses, the cause of justice marched on and they defeated the Tammeder Clan. In fact, the only Tammeder ship that was not destroyed was the mother ship...it disappeared during the final battle and it was never to be seen again."

"Gregorical, stop the recording," Micah said. "Tell me, did they ever find the Tammeder mother ship?"

"No, all traces of the Tammeder Clan disappeared with the mother ship. No one ever heard from them again," Gregorical said.

"That's strange. It doesn't make sense that they would give up like that." Micah looked at Hannelore to see if she agreed.

"I suppose it is strange. Gregorical, could the Tammeder Clan time travel?" Hannelore spoke into the air.

"No. Time travel was invented by the Armankouri people roughly two million years ago." Gregorical said. "You should finish watching the recording as the next section is important."

"Okay then," Micah said.

The presentation continued. "The known universe was divided into districts and they assigned each district to a group of Wardein. Each group was charged with guarding the peoples of their district from any evil. Anyone who would become a Warden was first required to pass vigorous training on the lifeless planet of Morolith. There they would hone their skills, relying on nothing more than their own wits, their own strength, and each other."

The presentation showed images of Wardein training on this hostile world as they faced life-threatening tests and battles. "Since then, the Wardein protected the people of the universe from the villains of the cosmos. In fact, after the defeat of the Tammeder, the Wardein went on the hunt for the Firebreathers. These people possessed the ability to project fire and ash from their mouths and devour people and sometimes whole towns."

"They sound like dragons," quipped Hannelore.

Images of the Wiskolo or the Firebreathers appeared on the screen and they looked much like what humans would call dragons. "The Firebreathers were a lizard-based life form from the planet Wiskol. They migrated away from the planet when it was destroyed by solar flares and for many millennia roamed the universe in search of a new home world. They often destroyed the native populations hoping to recreate the planet in the image of their beloved Wiskol.

"That's heart-breaking," said Hannelore. "I'm glad they don't exist anymore."

The recording continued. "The Firebreathers were engaged by the Wardein. Instead of destroying the Wiskolo, the Wardein found a new planet for them at the far reaches of the universe. This planet suited the needs of the Firebreathers well and they promised never to enter the realm of the peoples of the universe ever again."

"But we've seen dragons on Earth. Haven't we?" Hannelore looked away from the screen and held a finger up to her lips.

Micah piped up. "No Hannelore, they're a myth. It's a coincidence that the Firebreathers look like dragons." He rolled his eyes.

"No, it's entirely possible that a group of Firebreathers came to your world millions of years ago. Perhaps that's the source of your planet's legend. You must always be careful when dismissing something as impossible or as a myth. The universe is an enormous place, and no one knows all its secrets." Gregorical said.

"That's good advice, Micah. You should listen to it," said Hannelore as she glared at Micah.

Micah kept his mouth shut, but turned away to hide an eye roll.

* * *

Darbian and Taurean debated what to do and how to deal with Vinitor once they reached the Belt of Orion.

"I've got an idea," said Darbian. "If we deploy the Chrono drive, then we could freeze them in their tracks. That would buy us some much needed time, a lot of time."

Taurean perked up with excitement. "I think it would work. Create a time dilation field that would surround the whole ship and everyone in it. The people aboard would never be the wiser and we would have ample time to come up with a way to get the people off the ship. The only problem is that a Chrono drive can't be set to a timer. Someone would have to be in Vinitor's presence to activate it."

"That would be a problem," responded Darbian. "Perhaps we could create a remote device to activate it. I think I already have such an invention just about ready to go.

"But how will we fool him? He must know what a Chrono drive looks like." Taurean looked to Darbian for an answer as he had experience dealing with treacherous characters such as Vinitor.

"If we're quick about it, then we could pull it off. Maybe we could add a few parts to it to make it look like something it isn't. Vinitor isn't stupid, but he isn't the brightest star in the sky either. That might buy us enough time to activate it." Darbian thrust his hands together and rubbed them back and forth. His eyes grew wide and his voice hit a higher octave. The plan sounded like the perfect option to him.

Gregorical interrupted. "Gentlemen, if we disconnect the Chrono drive, then how will we reach the other Wardein for help? We won't be able to create wormholes or time travel in the slightest."

"I should have thought of that," said Darbian. He paced across the bridge once again.

Taurean whirled around in his chair. "We can get another Chrono drive at your base, can we not Darbian? All we have to do is travel that far. Will we have enough time?"

"We're quite far away. Gregorical, can you do the calculations for us?" Darbian put his hand over his chin.

Gregorical's navigation device beeped, squeaked, and then provided an answer. "We would have to increase the power on the Galacto drive to break the light speed barrier. It's 42 million light years from our current position."

"42 million light years!" Micah interrupted as he reentered the bridge.

Gregorical paused and then continued. "Ah yes, you've finished watching the presentation."

"How is it even possible to go so far?" Micah's mouth hung open.

Hannelore walked in behind him. "Darbian, I didn't thank you before for saving us."

"You're welcome, but there's no need to thank me." Darbian glanced back at the ceiling. "Gregorical, yes, 42 million light years. We'll be lucky not to burn out the Galacto drive."

"Sir, we must burn out the Galacto drive to travel that far with any brevity," Gregorical said.

"Thank you," Micah said in a very soft tone.

"What's that?" Darbian asked.

"I didn't thank you either. You and the other Wardein are heroes. I'm sorry for being angry with you earlier." Micah put his hands in his pockets and meandered up to Darbian.

"Don't worry about that. If I had just been snatched up from my planet with a bunch of strangers, I'd be angry too."

Darbian patted Micah on the shoulder. "What we have to worry about are the people that Vinitor has captured.

"What people?" Micah asked with a wrinkled brow.

"Yes, you weren't here for that part were you?" Darbian said. "Vinitor sent us a message that he's captured hundreds of your people. He's keeping them hostage aboard his ship in another sector not too far from here. It's time for us to be heroes again, Micah. I'll need your help and yours too, Hannelore. And I need you to have faith in me."

"Absolutely!" remarked Hannelore.

Micah nodded.

"With any luck, we won't be stranded in the recesses of space," Darbian said with a smile.

"Wait, what?" Micah blinked his eyes.

"To the Belt of Orion, Gregorical. If you're going to face danger, then you might as well do it headlong and with no help," Darbian spouted as he sat down.

"That doesn't make a lot of sense," Hannelore said as she plopped down right beside Darbian.

Darbian looked at her and put his hand on top of her head. "It's not supposed to."

CHAPTER 6

GREGORICAL and his passengers arrived shortly there-after at their destination.

The Belt of Orion an asteroid cluster that surrounded an entire star system. It was located in the heart of the Orion constellation and thus the name was given.

Hidden in the midst of the asteroid belt was Vinitor's command ship.

A crew member for the bounty hunter spoke. "Sir, the Warden's ship has shown up on our scanners. Shall I alert them to our presence?"

"No, let them think we're not here yet. I want to monitor them for a while and see if they have any tricks planned for us. It's imperative we acquire the Convergence this time. We don't have long before the device must be delivered," Vinitor said.

* * *

"Taurean, you finished altering the Chrono drive?" Darbian

asked as he operated the ship's scanners to search for Vinitor's ship.

"One more modification to make. The remote mechanism hasn't been cooperating. I would prefer more time to work on it, but we don't have that option." Taurean fiddled with the circuitry of the Chrono drive as he sat on the floor of the bridge.

"I don't understand," said Micah. "Why can't Gregorical grow another Chrono drive? Why do we have to go off without one?"

"It doesn't work like that, my friend," Darbian responded.

Gregorical spoke. "My ability to regenerate myself is limited to the basic ship parts and functions. The Chrono drive is a separate piece of technology. It was an addition to my body."

"Who made the Chrono drive?" Micah looked back at Darbian.

"My people invented the Chrono drive," said Taurean. "We gave the technology to the Wardein to assist their efforts."

"You'll find that a lot of the most impressive inventions in our universe came from the Armankouri. To say their scientists are geniuses is an understatement." Darbian went back to scanning.

"How are we going to rescue those people?" Hannelore asked while she looked out into the asteroid belt beyond.

"Haven't figured that one out yet, but the first thing we will do is find more Wardein. I think if we can surround Vinitor then we can force him to surrender," Darbian said. "I'm not sure that he's here yet. His ship does not appear on the sensors, but it's possible he's hiding behind an asteroid."

"One of us must meet him face to face to deploy the

device," Taurean put his hand over his wrist. "Oh dear, my heart is racing. It's up to 350 beats a minute and it should only be 270."

"Calm down, my friend. This plan will work. It has to." Darbian turned around to comfort Taurean.

"The Chrono drive is ready, Master Darbian." Taurean paused. "I think it should be me to meet Vinitor." He stood and put his hands together.

"Why do you say that?" Darbian walked over to Taurean. "You're not trained to defend yourself, Taurean. If something goes wrong, then you won't be able to fight your way out."

"I'm not concerned about that, Master Darbian. It's my fault that the rest of you are in this mess. It's my fault that those people are being held hostage on that ship. Besides, if something goes wrong, I can activate the Chrono drive manually while you and the children will be safe to proceed and find the Wardein." Taurean picked up the remote control.

"Taurean, whatever happens, be back aboard this ship before you activate the Chrono drive." Darbian's voice quickened.

"I'll be fine, Master Darbian." Taurean placed the remote control in his pocket. "If I'm still aboard Vinitor's ship when the device is activated, then no one will be the wiser. I'll be frozen in time along with the rest. Vinitor won't have time to attack me before you bring back the rest of the Wardein."

"I don't want to rescue you for a second time today. You better know what you're doing or I might leave you there," Darbian said with a wry smile.

"I must say that your confidence is inspiring, Master

Darbian." Taurean took a deep breath. "Let's contact Vinitor and tell him we're ready."

"Fine then. Gregorical, send a message and tell him we've arrived." Darbian walked over to the Chrono drive and placed his hand on it. "I sure hope you have it in you."

Gregorical contacted Vinitor and relayed their coordinates.

A few moments later, Vinitor's ship emerged from the asteroid belt, but something was amiss. The command ship had split into two pieces. They were flying side by side at first, but one section stopped as the other approached Gregorical.

"What is going on here?" Darbian looked back at Taurean. "I'll bet that the hostages were split up. Some in one part of the ship while the others and Vinitor himself are on the other. I didn't even know his ship could do that."

The bay door on the forward ship opened. The lights flashed inside inviting Darbian to bring his ship into the cargo bay for a meeting.

"Don't go inside Master Darbian. Send me inside an escape pod. Fire me and the Chrono drive right into the heart of the ship." Taurean grabbed Darbian's forearm. "I implore you sir."

Darbian shook his head. "That will not work, Taurean. For one, the ship has separated and the time dilation field won't be big enough to capture both ships inside. Second, if you go over there in a pod, how in Andromeda are you going to get back?"

"If you go inside the ship, then we'll be trapped. Vinitor will have no incentive to let us out again. We'd be forced to fight our way out, and we won't have time to activate the Chrono drive." Taurean turned his back and waved his hands about.

"Wait, I've got a plan. I'm not sure it's a good plan, but a bad plan is better than no plan," Darbian quipped.

"You have an odd way of looking at things," Micah piped up.

"Gregorical, fly us into the space between the two ships. Be quick about it," Darbian snapped.

Gregorical flew quickly to a point precisely between the two ships.

"Activate the tractor beam on the second ship. Pull it toward the first ship as fast as you can!" Darbian shouted.

"Sir, I doubt that our tractor beam is strong enough to pull the second ship very much at all," the artificial intelligence stated as if Darbian should know better.

"Yes, but it doesn't have to move very much. It just has to happen before we crash into the other ship." Darbian lowered his chin. The hairs on the back of his neck stood up straight. He gritted his teeth.

"Why would we crash into the other ship?" Micah leaped from sitting.

"Because we're going to hit the thrusters." Darbian cracked his knuckles.

"This doesn't sound like a bad plan. I'm demoting it to a horrible plan," Taurean said.

"Taurean, take the Chrono drive and get into one of the escape pods. Prepare to fire it," Darbian said.

"Working with the Wardein is not like a day in the lab." Taurean grabbed the Chrono drive, ran to the back of the ship, and entered one of the escape pods.

"Well, they didn't train me to be a scientist," Darbian said. "And I was never good at math."

"I hope Gregorical is good at math," Hannelore said.

Darbian whipped his head upward. "Gregorical, this

part is tricky. Fire the escape pod at the first ship and into the open bay!"

Gregorical did as he was told.

The pod fired, sputtered out of his bay, and entered Vinitor's ship. It bounced around the cargo hold, rolled over a few times, and came to rest amid several freight containers.

Darbian nodded. "Gregorical, fire the thrusters and prepare to take evasive maneuvers. On my mark!"

Gregorical engaged his thrusters and the force of both the engines and the tractor beam moved the other half of the command ship.

"We've got a few seconds before we're crushed between the two sections of that ship." Darbian tapped his fingers against the control panel.

"I don't make a habit of questioning you sir, but what next?" Gregorical said.

"Let Taurean do the work. He said he was willing to leave himself behind. He will have to do just that." Darbian spun on his feet and jogged to the central control panel. He pressed down on the communicator, closed his eyes, and spoke slowly. "Taurean, we're going to have to leave you behind."

Taurean paused as he was about to exit the pod. "Yes, I understand."

Micah ran up next to Darbian. "This is not a good idea!"

"Steady now, Micah," said Taurean. "There's always someone looking out for us even when we don't know it."

Micah grimaced.

Hannelore did the same. "That day...the day Travis was going to beat us up...that was Taurean who protected us. He shape-shifted into a cop."

"Be strong children," said Taurean.

"Taurean, I'll tell you when the two ships are close enough and you give me a two second warning to get out of here before you activate the Chrono drive. Got it?" Darbian spoke frantically.

"Yes, got it," Taurean said. "I'm getting out of the pod now."

Vinitor entered the cargo hold to open the pod and find what he hoped to be the Convergence.

Instead, Taurean popped out first.

"You again?" Vinitor thrashed his arms back and forth. "I'm absolutely sick of meeting miserable little creatures today. First it was the humans, then it was you, and then the Warden had to ruin my day. I would blow you all to atoms if I didn't want to get paid!"

"Master Vinitor, here is your promised item. I hope you use it wisely." Taurean pulled the Chrono drive out of the pod and set it on the floor of the cargo hold.

"That doesn't look like what you brought out back on Earth. And what is that blasted Warden doing? Bringing the two ships back together? Doesn't he know I keep my word? What are you up to?" Vinitor tilted his head to the side.

"Well, yes. I must admit that we haven't been completely honest with you." Taurean reached down and flipped on the Chrono drive, which was the first step to allowing the device to be activated remotely.

"That device...it looks like a Chrono drive!" The bounty hunter pointed at it with his staff.

"Well, that's because it is," Taurean quipped.

"Guards, destroy this pathetic, lying creature before he gives me a headache." Vinitor stepped out of the way.

The guards took aim, but, at that moment, Darbian

alerted Taurean that Vinitor's ships were now close enough to each other for the time dilation field to work.

"Go now, Master Darbian. No time to waste," Taurean spoke into his communicator.

"Fast Gregorical! Out of here! Now!" Darbian's voice cracked.

Taurean activated the time dilation field.

Gregorical shot upwards and away from the two ships.

The Chrono drive lit up and a wall of energy emanated from it in all directions. First Taurean froze in his tracks and then everyone else in the cargo hold. The bubble spread quickly.

Gregorical escaped by the plasma burning off from his engines as the wave of energy captured the other ship. Now both halves of the command ship were frozen in a pocket of time.

It trapped Taurean aboard and now he faced death from Vinitor's guards, but Darbian had the time he needed.

"Sir, the time dilation field has ceased expanding. We are clear of its effects," Gregorical said.

Darbian looked to the screen and saw the ships growing ever smaller in the distance. He stared at the sight. "Taurean, my friend, we return soon. I hope."

CHAPTER 7

GREGORICAL FLEW AWAY from the Belt of Orion. Within a few moments, the distance was so great that Vinitor's frozen ships were no longer detected.

"Gregorical, are your energy banks sufficiently charged for our next mission?" Darbian asked as he sat down and reclined in his chair.

"Is the destination Base 401, sir?" Gregorical replied in a quiet tone.

Darbian stared at the ceiling, his eyes fixed as though in a trance. "Yes, it's the closet one to our current position."

"Energy is sufficient, but there is no guarantee we will reach our destination safely. Might I suggest looking for another planet and synthesizing a Chrono drive there?" Gregorical ran a list of planets up on the main screen for Darbian to view.

Darbian folded his hands then broke one away to scratch his chin. "I like the idea, but we need to contact the other Wardein. The quickest way to do that is to get to the base. We have to risk the Galacto drive giving out. The odds of finding a planet nearby that will possess the technology to recreate a Chrono drive aren't high. That's why I was assigned to this sector after all...because the civilizations weren't that advanced."

Hannelore squirmed. "I don't understand, Darbian. Are you saying they gave you a low spot on the totem pole?"

"No, it's not like that. My scores in training were never that high. I was good enough to become a Warden, but they gave me a district they thought would be easier to handle. Little did they know what trouble I could get myself into." Darbian leaned up and stared through the children as though they weren't there.

"Are you okay, Darbian?" Micah noticed the look on Darbian's face and he needed Darbian to be confident.

"I left Taurean behind. He was willing to do it for our sakes, but I'm not sure I can bring him back," Darbian said.

Micah scowled. "What do you mean? Earlier, you both sounded like it wasn't that hard of a problem to fix."

Darbian sighed. "The time dilation field is easy to break with the right resources, sure. But..."

"But what?" Micah spat out.

"Something's wrong. Gregorical knows it. Taurean suspected it." Darbian opened his mouth as if to speak again, but no words came out.

"What are you talking about?" Hannelore folded her arms.

Darbian turned his back. "The Wardein should've responded by now. It's unusual that at least one of them wouldn't answer us. Highly unusual!"

"Maybe they're busy," Micah said.

"Do you know how I found you earlier today? Why I showed up on that planet even though no one there even can travel the stars? How did I know that you needed me?" Darbian rubbed his eyes.

Hannelore and Micah looked at each other.

"How?" said Micah.

"Because someone called for my help. I don't know who it was or how they did it, but someone from Earth alerted us to what was happening." Darbian said. "And so..."

Micah grew more confused by the minute.

Hannelore sat back down.

"I came. I showed up because that's what Wardein do. We respond when someone needs us, no questions asked," Darbian said.

"So why didn't the others come?" Micah sunk in his chair.

"Exactly," responded Darbian.

Hannelore shrugged her shoulders. "So what do we do?"

Darbian got up and walked to the main control panel. He bent over it and then turned back to the children. "I'm not sure you should place your trust in me."

"Sir, now is not the time to second guess ourselves. Taurean is depending upon us. The hostages are depending upon us. The children are depending upon you," Gregorical said.

"Under different circumstances, I might just detour to another planet and see if we couldn't manufacture another Chrono drive." Darbian grimaced. "But I can't shake the feeling we have a bigger problem on our hands. We need to get to Base 401 as soon as possible."

"Children, you need to secure yourselves in a seat," Gregorical said.

Darbian strapped himself in. "Gregorical, set a course for Base 401."

"So I take it this will be bumpy?" Hannelore smiled. "I've always been a big fan of roller coasters."

"Assuming we don't get stranded in space, yeah, it will be a lot like that," Darbian responded.

Micah's eyes got big.

Gregorical activated the Galacto drive and pointed the ship in the right direction to traverse the 42 million light years to Base 401. The engines on Gregorical's stern section lit up and brightened the dark space around them. They fired and the ship was off.

To reach the base in a timely manner, the Galacto drive would have to operate at full capacity. It would surely burn out if it maintained high speeds for more than a few minutes, but those very minutes were precious.

Gregorical rattled as the engines became unstable. "Sir, we have a problem. I don't think we can hold this speed for long. The trip should take approximately seven minutes and I think we have five at the most."

"Hold it together old friend." Darbian said as he gripped the control panel. "If need be, turn off other functions to protect the engines."

Gregorical flew not just rapidly but recklessly. It was impossible to travel from the Belt of Orion to Base 401 in a straight line and so Gregorical made course adjustments every fraction of a second to avoid hitting stars, planets, and nebulas alike. The ship shifted directions faster that the human mind could comprehend. Up, down, sideways, and straight.

"I must disable the gravity field," Gregorical said. "The energy is needed elsewhere."

Darbian nodded.

Micah held his breath.

Hannelore smiled.

"Go ahead!" shouted Darbian.

The gravity field turned off and a sense of weightlessness came over every passenger. They floated in their seats and fell back down again. No roller coaster on Earth could deliver such sensations.

"I'm going to throw up," Micah said. He placed both hands over his mouth.

"This is incredible!" screamed Hannelore.

Gregorical twisted, turned, and spun his way into deep space, far beyond the realm of any nearby galaxy. Most of the trip was complete now and a small object hung in space before them, reflecting the light of a million distant galaxies.

The engines were rocking back and forth within the hull of the ship.

An alarm sounded and echoed an ear-piercing high-pitched tone. "Hull compromised. Hull compromised. Ship is in danger of disintegrating. Ship is in danger of disintegrating," sounded the voice of an automated alert program rather than Gregorical himself.

"Darbian, are we going to be okay?" shouted Hannelore

"I hope so!" responded Darbian.

"I need a bag!" shouted Micah.

"Sir, the journey is almost complete. I'll deactivate the engines immediately. The deceleration process, however, may be compromised by damage to the hull. It's unknown if we can slow down before ramming the base," Gregorical said.

"Why didn't you think of that before? I thought you were supposed to be a brilliant super computer?" Darbian was exhausted with the bumpy trip and unusually sarcastic.

"Sir, you didn't ask," responded Gregorical.

Darbian tried grabbing a hold of the circular panel in front of him. "Can you decelerate Gregorical?"

"Making an attempt now, sir," Gregorical said.

"Why don't you set a course to orbit the base until you can slow down Gregorical? That way, we don't head straight for it," Micah said despite his impending vomit.

"That's...that's brilliant young man." Darbian tried to alter the settings on the reverse thrusters, the devices used to slow down the craft when the Galacto drive was in use. "Gregorical, change your course so that we assume an orbit."

Gregorical decelerated himself as best as he could manage and entered an orbit of the base, albeit a dangerously quick orbit.

"You can turn the gravity field back on. We need to get to the communicators," Darbian said while gripping the panel with every ounce of his strength.

They heard an energy fluctuation.

"Absolutely sir. Gravity field reestablished," Gregorical said.

Darbian and the children plopped down into their chairs.

"Oh, thank goodness," exclaimed Micah.

"Can we do that again on the trip back, Darbian?" Hannelore was giddy.

"My dear, with any luck, I'll never have to do that again for the rest of my life," responded Darbian as he walked to the communicator. "This is Warden Darbian of the 401st Sector. We require assistance from any Warden present. As you may see, we're in orbit of the station. We're unable to slow down and dock, however. We require immediate aid."

There was no response from the base.

"Where could they be?" Darbian's swallowed his heart.

Gregorical replied. "Sir, I detect no other ships in the area."

Hannelore pouted. "Is that weird?"

"Very," said Gregorical.

"Children, I'm afraid we'll have to enter the station from the outside," Darbian said as he hung his head.

"What do you mean?" Micah asked as he forced himself up from his sickness-induced stupor.

"We'll have to put on spacesuits and take a spacewalk to the base. It's the only way we will get aboard and figure out what's going on." Darbian walked to the teleportation room. "Follow me, children."

Micah moaned. "Spacesuits? Spacewalking? I've had enough roller coasters for the day. When is this going to end?"

"Oh, come on, you dork. This is the adventure of a lifetime. How can you be so scared of it?" Hannelore leapt to follow Darbian.

"It's not that I'm scared. I never said I was scared. I just appreciate walking on the ground in a whole new way after today." Micah followed although a bit more slowly.

Darbian stopped walked and pursed his lips. "Gregorical, do you think we have any spacesuits that would fit the children?"

"Yes, I believe so. There are a few made for the standard Armankouri size. These should fit the children albeit loosely." Gregorical opened one of his closets to reveal the suits.

"Okay children. Put them on. We need to get going. We'll be ready to teleport in a moment. I have to make sure we appear far enough away from the ship so we don't get caught in its gravity." Darbian put on his spacesuit.

Micah put his suit on, but stopped. "I don't understand. If we're using the teleporter then why can't we just teleport aboard the base?"

"It doesn't work like that. The teleporter only works to get us on or off the ship. It can't teleport us through other objects which means other ships or stations." Darbian put his helmet on. "Time is wasting."

"What if Hannelore and I just stay here? Do you really need us out there? Isn't it kind of dangerous to be flying through open space like that?" Micah stood with his helmet in hand.

Darbian turned back around. "It would be better if you came with me. If you stay aboard Gregorical, then I won't be able to come back and get you. Spacewalking to a stationary object is one thing, catching up with a ship that's flying near the speed of light is just not possible."

"Yeah, but staying with Gregorical wouldn't be bad. We're safe here," replied Micah.

Darbian raised his eyebrow. "Normally, I wouldn't mind leaving you with Gregorical, but he needs repair. If the tractor beam aboard the station doesn't work, then you could be stranded out here for some time. There's nothing to worry about. Once you're aboard the station, you'll be safe."

Micah shuffled his feet. "Yeah, but isn't there debris floating through space and all that? What if we get hit?"

"Boy, what are you afraid of?" Darbian said.

"Your dad, right?" Hannelore said.

Micah tensed up. "Maybe I am afraid. What's so bad about that?"

"What about your dad?" Darbian said.

Hannelore looked to the floor.

Micah gulped. "My dad died in space. I saw it happen. I don't want us to end up like that."

Darbian walked over and stooped down to Micah's eye level. "I'm sorry, I didn't know."

"His ship blew up," Micah responded.

"Nothing will happen to us Micah. Out here, there is no

debris. I promise you I won't put you in any danger. I'm here to protect you and Hannelore and I always will be." Darbian put his hand on Micah's shoulder.

"That's what my dad said. He said he would always be there." Tears streamed down from Micah's eyes. "Then he wasn't."

Darbian's eyes were watery. "Micah, I didn't know your dad, but I know you. You're brave and so I think your dad must have been brave too."

"He was," said Micah.

"What happened to your dad was terrible and sometimes bad things happen, but don't let that stop you from moving forward. You have a big life ahead of you and there will be lots of challenges ahead. And it's ok to be afraid sometimes, but don't let that keep you from living." Darbian took his finger and pointed to Micah's heart. "The world needs Micah. Don't shrink back from it."

"You're going to protect us?" Micah bit his lower lip.

"With my life," replied Darbian.

Micah put his helmet on and snapped it closed.

Darbian nodded.

"Are you prepared to teleport, sir?" Gregorical asked.

Darbian attached himself to the both of the children with a tether. "Ready to go."

Gregorical operated the teleporter and placed them halfway between the station and the ship.

Darbian's suit was equipped with a thruster that would help the three navigate the gap between where they began and the airlock to the station. He fired the thruster, and the three were off.

Suddenly, the tether attached to Hannelore broke, and she drifted away from the others.

"Guys, guys, help me!" Hannelore cried.

"Micah, hold on. If we don't get her back now then she may drift beyond our reach," Darbian said.

Micah turned around to look for Hannelore. "Get Gregorical to teleport her back aboard!"

"Something I didn't tell you. He's only programmed to lock onto my signal. Anyone teleporting with me must be nearby in order for him to lock on. We must get close to her!" Darbian slammed his thumb on the button that activated the thruster.

Hannelore drifted faster and faster away

"Guys!" cried Hannelore. "Hurry! It feels like something is pulling me away!"

CHAPTER 8

HANNELORE SPED up as she drifted further and further away from Darbian and Micah. The night was black, and she was disappearing into the darkness.

Darbian pounded on the control for the thrusters, but they weren't reducing the distance.

"Hannelore, can you hear us?" Micah shouted into his helmet.

"Yes, but I can barely see you. Aren't you coming for me?" Hannelore cried.

"We can't catch up at this speed Hannelore," Darbian said.

"What about the station Darbian? Does the station have a teleporter? What if we turned around and went inside?" Micah growled.

"Don't you leave me out here!" Hannelore thrashed her arms.

Darbian winced. "Wouldn't do any good, my boy. The only teleporters are on the Wardein ships."

"What about a tractor beam? The station has one of those, right?" Micah clamored.

"Yes, but it's short range only. She'll be gone before we can activate it," Darbian prattled.

Suddenly, a door opened in the middle of the vastness. A bright yellow light shone out from the opening.

It drew Hannelore inside, and the door shut behind her.

"Well, I didn't expect that," said Darbian.

"Where is she, Darbian?" Micah gloomed.

"She's where we'll be in a moment. Don't worry Micah. There's another ship here, but it's cloaked. Hannelore was drawn in with a tractor beam and I imagine that beam is about to grasp us as well." Darbian took his hand off the thruster controls.

The tractor beam took a hold of Darbian and Micah and drew them faster and faster toward the same spot where Hannelore disappeared behind the mysterious door.

In a moment, the door opened again, and it took inside Darbian and Micah. The door closed behind them and they landed not so gracefully on the floor of the ship.

Hannelore stood nearby and with hands on hips.

Darbian rolled onto his back.

Micah tried to stand up.

"Some rescue attempt, you two. Some stupid ship kidnaps me and the best you can do is get caught too?" Hannelore tapped her foot repeatedly.

"My dear, the reason we couldn't catch you is that a tractor beam from this ship was pulling you aboard. My thruster had no chance of catching you." Darbian sat up. "Don't worry, though. We're safe here. This is a Warden's ship, and we are now guests."

"Beginning airlock procedure," a voice spoke in the background.

The sound of air flowing from vents filled their ears. Soon there was enough oxygen for the trio to remove their helmets. An invisible shield dropped all around them with the sound of sparks and the sight of flashes of light.

"I recognize this ship," said Darbian. "It belongs to Aculpus Atronis, an old friend. The question is where is he?"

They heard moaning echoing off the walls of the ship. First, it was soft, but it became louder.

Darbian put his arm behind him and motioned to the children. "Stay here." He slowly climbed up a flight of stairs. With every step, the sound of moaning grew louder. He reached the top of the stairs and a door automatically opened. Darbian entered, and the door closed behind him.

"How long should we wait for him?" Hannelore asked.

"There might be some sort of monster up there. We should wait until he calls us up there. I'm tired of surprises," Micah said.

In the room above, Darbian searched through a mostly dark room as a few emergency lights flickered on and off. "What in the world happened here? Aculpus! Where are you? Are you here?"

The moaning turned to coughing, and, for a moment, sounded like garbled speech.

Darbian walked toward the sound. "Aculpus, is that you?"

"Darbian, I'm over here," a tempered voice answered back.

"Aculpus! What in the black abyss happened here?" Darbian said.

"Darbian, are the lights working?" Aculpus asked.

Darbian looked up with only an occasional flash shining upon his face. "No, can you turn them on?"

"Computer, turn the lights on," Aculpus stated.

"Ship's energy is at 34% capacity. Do you still wish to use full lighting?" A digitized voice answered back.

"Yes computer, turn them on," Aculpus shook his head.

Most of the lights on the ship came on and Darbian saw Aculpus for the first time in a long time.

Aculpus could not return the favor, however, as his race was blind. Where you might have eyes on most humanoids, Aculpus had a second set of ears. His skin was light brown, and he was mostly bald except for what would pass for a beard among his people, the Milinauks. Though they could not perceive light, Aculpus and his people had the rather remarkable ability of natural radar. Every Milinauk brain projected an energy signal that bounced off of objects and returned to be received by the mind. So in a manner of speaking, they saw the world around them quite well.

"Your arm! Your uniform is tattered. What happened to you?" Darbian stooped down to tend to his friend.

Aculpus was laying down with his right arm in a sling. "The battle didn't go well, Darbian."

"What battle? How did you end up here? Why is the ship cloaked?" Darbian's heart pounded.

"Cloaked?" Aculpus tried to sit up too quickly and smacked his head on the ceiling above. "Bah! My ears! No wonder the power is so low. Computer, turn off the invisibility cloak. We don't need it here." He relaxed.

"Aculpus, what battle are you talking about?" Darbian went back to the subject at hand.

Aculpus raised himself up. "Don't you know, Darbian? Halinkoy...Halinkoy defeated us."

Darbian was silent, motionless.

"Darbian, they're all gone. The Wardein are defeated. I've never seen anything like it. If I survive this, I'll never know anything like it again." Aculpus laid back down.

"What do you mean they're gone? What happened to the Central Command?" Darbian massaged his chin.

Aculpus moaned again. "It's gone, Darbian. I barely made it out. I was late arriving to the battle and there was such destruction before me. No one could have convinced me to believe it if I had not been there. I don't want to believe it now, but it's true. Halinkoy's ships were too strong for me to salvage anything or anyone. They almost destroyed me. I put the ship on autopilot and told it to fly to the nearest unaffected base. I suppose it brought me to yours, Darbian?"

"Halinkoy, that name again. Why have I never heard of the Halinkoy Cult until today? I don't understand." Darbian paced around the room.

The children popped in from around the corner.

"Darbian, there aren't any monsters in here are there?" Hannelore quivered.

"No my dear, the monsters are far from here," Darbian said.

"Darbian, what's wrong, and who's that?" Micah pointed toward Aculpus.

Darbian stopped and looked at his friend. "This is my old friend, Aculpus Atronis of District 7822. He's a Warden like me and he's going to help us."

All four of Aculpus' ears perked up. "Help you do what exactly?"

"First thing, my friend, dock this ship with the station. We need to get Gregorical back up and running.

"Certainly! Computer, dock with the nearest station and begin a download of any new information." Aculpus sat up. "Darbian, what else can I do?"

Darbian turned to face him. "We need to get you aboard

the station and get you healed. Then we'll worry about what comes next."

The ship docked with the Warden station.

Base 401 was egg-shaped as though its makers started out building a sphere and changed their mind halfway through. It was white like an egg too with bright lights emanating from the upper and lower ends. The station itself was the brightest thing in the sky. All the nearby galaxies looked like dim blobs of light by comparison.

There were four spires pointing out from around the equator of the massive structure. Each designed to provide multiple docking stations, they were tube-like and set equal distances apart.

Aculpus' ship approached one. It connected with a thud and everyone walked onto the station.

"Safety never felt so good," said Darbian.

* * *

Darbian helped Aculpus into the infirmary.

Meanwhile, the children climbed up ladders and played with innocent looking devices.

The Warden station was a magnificent sight for the children. There were high ceilings and scaffolding all along the walls. There were catwalks above that connected work-stations to doors, each with an oculus for an opening. The floors and walls were spotless.

In fact, the children noticed their reflections on all the surfaces if they stood close enough.

"Micah, these steps float through the air!" Hannelore exclaimed.

"Now, how would you know that?" Micah turned

around in time to see Hannelore riding a craft from one side of the station to the other.

She stood behind a small podium that luckily included a few levers to control where she was going. That didn't keep her from banging into a few walls along the way though.

Micah rolled his eyes. "Hannelore, come down from there! You'll break something!"

"Oh, it's fine! Darbian will get me down when he comes back. Stop worrying and have a little fun." Hannelore punched a button here and there just to find out what would happen.

"I don't want to have fun," Micah said under his breath. "I want everything to be normal again." Micah took a seat on the floor and folded his legs. He stared at the ceiling and noticed a wide set of windows near the top of the large hall they were in. He climbed up and looked out.

After a moment of scaling the scaffolding, Micah reached an observation deck.

A ring of windows stretched all around the station.

One had the ability to look in any direction. There wasn't much to view, however, as Micah soon found out.

He placed his hands on the glass, at least he thought it was glass, and peered out into the cosmos. "Where do you think Earth is?" Micah glared toward the brightest blob of light in the sky.

"I don't know. Does it matter? I thought you wanted to be an astronaut. You're getting your wish. You're getting to see the stars and lots of things neither of us ever imagined. And wait a minute; didn't you say a while ago that you wanted to be here? What changed your mind?" Hannelore floated up to the observation deck and sat her craft down next to him.

Micah's face lit up. "How did you get up here?"

Hannelore hopped off the steps. "I told you I knew what I was doing."

"You can't really see anything out the window," Micah whispered.

"Is going home all you can think about? Why you're so worried? When Darbian comes back and fixes Gregorical, he'll probably take us home then. Vinitor can't get to us anymore. There's no need to keep looking out for us now." Hannelore stretched her back and stared out the window herself.

"Don't you understand what's going on, Hannelore? Everybody's in danger. The people on Vinitor's ship; what about them? The Wardein won't respond to Darbian. Aculpus was in some kind of fight and apparently lost. Something is going on and they don't want to tell us yet." Micah scowled.

"You worry too much," responded Hannelore.

"Besides, it's not that I want to go home, although I want to tell my mom about everything that's happened. I'm just tired of being in trouble. This isn't what I meant when I said I wanted to be an astronaut." Micah bowed his head and then looked out the window again.

"Everything will be fine. Darbian will take care of us. And if not, then I'll take care of you!" Hannelore put her hands on her hips and posed as though she were some cape-wearing superhero. She laughed.

"I don't need you to take care of me!" Micah quipped.

"Sure you do. We take care of each other. That's what friends do." Hannelore smiled.

"Well, I'll hold you to that then," replied Micah.

"I hope you do. And you better take care of me too, mister! Don't think you're getting off easy." Hannelore put her face up against the window and made faces at the universe. She laughed.

"What are you laughing at?" Micah's mood had lightened a little.

"We're seeing things people haven't seen before. I can't help but be happy about it."

Micah shook his head. "I hope you never change."

CHAPTER 9

DARBIAN EMERGED FROM THE INFIRMARY. "Children, where are you?"

Both kids shouted, "Up here!"

"Ah, you've made use of the levitators. Come down. I want you to help me bring Gregorical in for repair." Darbian walked to a workstation in the middle of the room with a design similar to the one on his own ship.

Hannelore rode the levitator she had just mastered while Micah took a set of stairs he didn't see earlier.

Darbian pushed a few buttons on the control panel and spoke. "Gregorical, are you there?"

"Yes, sir, I was becoming worried. I thought you would have made contact earlier." Gregorical's voice piped through the speakers in the hall.

"Yes, our entry into the station didn't quite go as planned, but I've met up with Aculpus Atronis." Tears welled up in Darbian's eyes. "Unfortunately, he was injured, but now he's in the infirmary and we can focus on getting you back in shape."

"Sir, pardon me, but you sound worried," Gregorical responded.

"My friend..." Darbian said.

"Aculpus was injured in battle?" Gregorical's somber tone bounced off the walls like an echo.

"Yes." Darbian clenched his fist and spoke. "The Wardein aren't here. They're gone. According to Aculpus, they're all gone. We're all that's left."

Gregorical was silent for a moment. "How is that possible?"

"Halinkoy," Darbian responded.

Gregorical replied. "You once told me you feared this day, but we will face it together. You are not alone."

Darbian leaned over the panel with his head bowed. "Next stop is Crystal Dawn and the Council of Planets."

"Are we going home soon?" Micah asked.

Darbian looked at him. "Children, I don't want to make you afraid, but I must tell you the truth. You are now in more peril than you can imagine. It's best you stay with me for now."

Hannelore blinked. "You can protect us right?"

"That's what they trained me to do," responded Darbian.

"Ready to engage sir," Gregorical said.

Darbian stared at the panel. "Initiating tractor beam, ready to bring you into the shop."

Micah looked at Hannelore then turned his eyes to Darbian. "Well, when will it be safe?"

"Until I can figure out how Halinkoy knew the Convergence was on Earth, then it's too dangerous to go back. He might go looking for it himself and there's no telling what or who he might find if he starts turning over stones. Can't

leave you here either. You must stay with me until then."
Darbian squeezed a lever to activate the tractor beam.

From the lower section of the station, a beam of energy
shot out into space. A series of concentric circles of light
vibrated through the beam until they reached their target,
Gregorical.

Gregorical slowed down.

The lower section of the station opened as Gregorical
retracted into the bay.

A series of tubes and wires sprung forth from the walls
and connected to the ship as the doors below closed
behind him.

"Sir, I believe I am docked," Gregorical said.

"I'll be in to see you shortly, old man," Darbian
responded.

Hannelore came up behind Darbian. "I don't understand. What did you fear would happen?"

"It's hard to explain. I don't really know what to make of
it myself." Darbian looked at the children and tapped his
fingers on the panel. "Two sets of memories...as long as I
can remember, I've always had them. It feels like I've lived
two different lives, very different lives." He walked away
from the panel and toward a door leading to an elevator.

"We're coming with you," Micah said.

"Well, that was the plan." Darbian managed a smile.

The three of them entered the elevator and jetted down
several dozen floors until they reached the bay where
Gregorical was docked.

Hannelore worked up the courage to ask the obvious
question. "I don't understand what you mean. How can you
remember two different lives?"

"I've been alone on this station all my life. As a young
man, I came here and have done nothing but walk these

lonely halls. I remember sitting on the floor and using the wormhole generator to view a hundred different worlds. I saw each of them many times, always wishing I could be a part of life somewhere and sometime. Rarely leaving, always looking in on the worlds that fascinated me most... including yours." Darbian extended a bridge to Gregorical's outer door.

The bridge moved out from under the deck where the three were standing. It zig-zagged around the tubes and wires until it reached the hull of Gregorical.

Darbian walked across the bridge, and the children followed.

"But I thought you said you were a Warden, and that you had been around the universe and that you saved people and defeated all sorts of villains?" Hannelore marveled.

"That's the crazy thing. I remember a completely different life as a Warden, a genuine Warden who traveled around more than he stood still. Facing foes, fighting, winning; I remember it all and I remember the camaraderie with my fellow Wardein. We lived here, trained here. Sometimes we went on missions together. Other times we were solo, but always in contact." Darbian paused as he waited to enter Gregorical's airlock.

"What else do you remember? Why did Gregorical say you feared this day was coming?" Micah asked the question that Hannelore had been hinting at.

Darbian stared off into space at first, but then looked at the children. "I remember a day when all the Wardein disappeared. Don't ask me how. I don't understand what it all means, but it's as though I've lived this day before. Yet, it came as a total shock when Aculpus told me what happened. I didn't want to believe what I heard, but in a way I was expecting it. I know that doesn't make any sense, but that's what happened." Darbian entered Gregorical's airlock.

The three walked about the ship.

Gregorical gave specific instructions on the damaged parts while Darbian did an expert job in repairing him.

The children assisted by passing along tools and placing their hands into small spaces that Darbian couldn't reach.

The tubes outside were feeding Gregorical with the elements necessary to rebuild his Galacto drive and a new Chrono drive. Soon, Gregorical would be in prime shape again.

"I feel brand new, sir. I don't believe I had ever been in worse shape. Being inside the Distortion Detector might not have been any worse. My circuits severely needed revamping." Gregorical commented.

Darbian paused. "The Distortion Detector. The Distortion Detector!" He dropped his tools and ran outside the ship.

Naturally, the children followed and barely got inside the elevator before Darbian closed the doors.

"What's a Distortion Detector?" Micah exclaimed.

It rushed them back to the nerve center of the base.

Upon departing the elevator, Darbian ran to the back of the room where he found a large green lever. He pulled it down and awaited the results.

The silvery, shiny metal wall of the station slowly divided in half. Beyond the bounds of the wall stood a large cylinder. The cylinder was clear and one could see through to find a peculiar item. A translucent sphere floated inside the cylinder. It had a green tinge, resembling a planet with its bumpy features and mismatched layout, but it was a machine, nonetheless.

"That's a Distortion Detector," said Darbian. He approached it slowly not wishing to disturb it. He put both hands on the cylinder and stared at the sphere within. "There's something...something very wrong."

Hannelore gaped at the object. "What does it do?"

Darbian looked back at the children. "This is a Distortion Detector. It doesn't exist within space and time. We can see it, but we could never touch or examine it. At best, we would ruin the device. At worst, it could ruin us. It works because it's not bound by time. It sees the changes, the movements. It detects shifts like a seismograph. We see the shifts and use that knowledge to fix what's been broken."

Micah smirked. "Okay, that's impressive."

Darbian stared. "It tells us times and places. Everything that happens in time and space leaves a fingerprint on this device. That's how it's supposed to work, but this isn't like anything I've ever seen. What I'm about to tell you is the source of our present problems, I believe. Something unspeakable has happened and I'm not sure what it was yet. I do know someone has ripped open the space-time continuum like a bag of popcorn. And whatever events put this into motion began on Earth."

"Earth?" asked Micah.

"Yes, and I've been suspecting that for a while. Taurean told me about a man named Ajax Halinkoy. You heard me say his name earlier, but you weren't there when Taurean told me the story." Darbian turned back to the children. "A human who had become a great enemy of the Armankouri people. I had never even heard of him, but Taurean said Halinkoy was a time traveler. Something odd had to have taken place on Earth for there to be a time traveler at all on such a planet. Something more odd yet for that time traveler to become a great menace to the most brilliant people in the universe. It took me a while to put two and two together, but I realized something a moment ago. The reason I have two sets of memories..."

"What? What's the reason?" shouted Hannelore.

Darbian continued to examine the Distortion Detector. "This Halinkoy is more than a time traveler. He's a villain like nothing I've ever seen before. Some way, somehow, he set off a Time Bomb."

"A time bomb? That doesn't seem like a huge deal," Micah retorted.

"No, no, I don't mean a simple explosive with a timer. I'm talking about a bomb that rips open time and space itself. They were rumored to exist during the ancient times, products of mad scientists. But no one knows. No good records of such events. The space-time continuum wasn't understood then. It's probably not completely understood now, but you get my point." Darbian shuttered. "Somehow, this Halinkoy has come across such a device and he's already used it."

"How do we stop this? How do we beat him?" Hannelore shouted.

"I'm not sure, but I know who would. We have to go to the Council of Planets immediately. It's not a short trip. We'll have to use the wormhole generator. Children, help me get Aculpus to the ship. We'll leave on Gregorical in the next few minutes. Hopefully, we're not too late." Darbian rushed back to the infirmary.

The children followed.

"But what can the Council do if there are no Wardein?" Micah said.

"They can call for help...to anyone who's listening," Darbian replied.

CHAPTER 10

"ACULPUS, my friend, we have to leave immediately!" Darbian shouted as he entered the room.

Aculpus tried lifting himself up on his elbows. "To where? What are you going on about?"

Darbian walked over to a counter and pulled out a syringe. "Stellar City. We need the advice of the Council. I suspect that our enemy has set off a Time Bomb. That's how he beat the Wardein so easily. He made it so they never existed. It makes sense now. I have two sets of memories and the only explanation is that I've lived two different lives, one in service to the Wardein and the other in a universe devoid of their presence. These two universes are tangled up together like fishing nets. Some way we have to put everything right again, but we need help. The science is out of our league." Darbian took the syringe and filled it with a healing serum called Meticulo.

"I think it will take more than a miracle drug to heal my wounds. If I am to enter any battles soon, then I'll need complete restoration and that means time under the Regenerative Shield...perhaps even a couple of days," Aculpus said.

"This may be a temporary solution, but it's the best we can do. We have to speak with the Council and we must prepare to engage Halinkoy." Darbian took the syringe and injected Aculpus with the Meticulo. "With any luck, we can leave you with the Council doctors and it shouldn't take them long to restore you."

Aculpus breathed in. "I do feel better now. Are we taking the children with us?"

"Yes, their planet isn't safe. That's a long story." Darbian put away the medicine.

"I must fly my own ship. We may need extra firepower if a battle commences." Aculpus stood up.

Darbian turned around and looked at his old friend. "Are you up to it? You're certainly welcome to come aboard Gregorical."

"Yes, I believe it is necessary. If need be, I can help protect the children if you and Gregorical need to engage in a fight." Aculpus walked to the closet to retrieve his armor.

"That's a good point. I hadn't thought of that. If there is a battle though, we'll need a lot more than two ships," Darbian said.

Aculpus put on his armor. "I don't think attacking Halinkoy head on with numbers would be in our favor as it stands. Remember, he defeated nearly the entire corps of Wardein. We must be smart rather. Strength alone won't win the day. This foe is like no other we've faced before."

"You're right. Brains, not brawn. Not exactly my style, I have to admit." Darbian stood at attention.

Aculpus raised his chin. "What's all that?"

Darbian cleared his throat. "My weapons are ready. My heart is prepared. I'm glad I have a friend like you by my side. No one should go into battle alone and if I am to die, I could choose no better ally."

Aculpus placed his hand on Darbian's shoulder. "Thank you, Darbian, but let's not speak of death just yet."

Darbian smiled. "When I board Gregorical, I'll send word ahead to the Council we'll be arriving soon," he said as he turned to leave the room.

Aculpus straightened his back. "Good. I've been looking forward to seeing the Stellar City again for a long time, although I wish it were under different circumstances. Let us be on our way."

With that, the two walked out of the infirmary, gathered the children, and boarded their respective ships.

Darbian took his place in front of the main screen. "Gregorical, are you ready to fly?"

"Absolutely sir," Gregorical replied.

"Move out when you're ready and send a message to the Council that we require their assistance," Darbian said.

"The Council has been notified." Gregorical lowered himself away from the docking station and left Base 401.

Aculpus' ship followed.

"Gregorical, open a wormhole. We're going to Stellar City." Darbian folded his hands behind his back.

Micah spoke up, "So you can just create wormholes whenever you want?"

"Yes, it's how we travel such great distances with relative speed," Darbian replied.

"You mean without blowing up the engines?" Hannelore added.

Darbian paused, turned back around, looked at her, and said, "Yes, without blowing up the engines."

"Work your magic Gregorical!" Hannelore shouted.

From the base of Gregorical's bow came a beam of

energy. It was orange and looked thick as a liquid. In fact, the beam swirled through space as though it were liquid. A few meters from the ship, however, the beam stopped in mid-space. It amassed into a ball of light that throbbed backward and forward and then upward as though it were breathing.

Suddenly the ball exploded and in its wake was a portal to another region of the universe, many billions of light years away. The edges of the portal were transparent, but it appeared as though space itself was flowing in two different directions. Inside the portal, one could see an entirely different set of stars. Outside the portal, it appeared as though space had been reduced to a pool of water running off the edges of a cliff.

"The wormhole is open, sir," said Gregorical.

Gregorical and all those aboard went through the wormhole and instantly traveled to a faraway galaxy, Crystal Dwelling.

It was a galaxy filled to the brim with blue stars, but few habitable worlds.

Darbian gazed at the blue hue of the galaxy. "It's beautiful."

"Wow, it really is," said Micah.

"Set a course for Crystal Dawn," Darbian said.

"I thought we were going to Stellar City?" asked Hannelore.

"Yes, but Stellar City is found on the planet of Crystal Dawn. Do you know why they call it that?" Darbian raised his eyebrows.

"I don't have any idea," responded Hannelore.

Darbian cracked a smile. "You'll see soon enough. In the center of the galaxy, the stars are so close together that the light prevails over everything. There is no deep, dark void of space there."

Hannelore looked off to the side and then back at Darbian with a glimmer in her eye. "I can't wait to see it."

Gregorical flew with immense speed toward the center of the galaxy.

Gregorical spoke up, "Sir, was Aculpus Atronis not following us?"

"He didn't follow us through the wormhole? Something's wrong. We have to get to Stellar City!" Darbian sat down, put his hands together, and placed them under his chin.

"We will arrive soon, sir," Gregorical stated.

"What's wrong? Why didn't Aculpus follow us?" Micah asked.

"I'm not sure why, but we need the help of the Council more than ever." Darbian walked out of the room.

"You said Aculpus was your friend. Is he a good man?" Micah pondered aloud.

Darbian whipped back around. "Of course he's a good man. There's no such thing as a bad Warden. Aculpus is a hero among the Wardein."

"It is weird he wouldn't follow us when he said he would," Hannelore said.

"Perhaps there's a good reason for that," Darbian replied.

Gregorical spoke. "Sir, we've received no communication from Aculpus Atronis stating the reason he did not follow."

Darbian straightened his back. "The Battle of Klimopira."

"I remember it well," said Gregorical.

"Well, you have to tell us the story," Micah said.

Darbian shifted back to the center of the room. "Many years ago, the planet of Klimopira was under attack by the Vengals, a warrior race that spent most of their history conquering planets for natural resources. The Klimopirans were a peaceful people, so they dispatched a squadron of Wardein to repel the Vengals. I had never been in battle before, not true battle. I had always faced off against a single foe or a roving gang of marauders. This was different. The Vengals spent much of their life learning the arts of war and hand-to-hand combat. I was inexperienced, but had the task of defending the capital city. This was the last hope of the Klimopirans. Their city would have to stand or their planet would fall."

"What happened next?" Hannelore implored.

Somber in his speech as he recounted the details of the battle, Darbian continued, "I was to defend the city alongside seven other Wardein. We were outmatched though. Thousands of Vengal warriors landed on the outskirts of the city. They were protected from above by several dozen starships, which attacked from the air while troops on the ground armed with cannons would plow their way to the president's quarters. Vengal starships decimated most of the city's defenses. The only line of defense left was us...the Wardein."

The children looked on.

Darbian continued with his story. "We each took to our ships to attack the Vengal spacecraft, but one by one each Warden was downed or destroyed until only I was left. Gregorical and I were preparing ourselves to be destroyed. We barely made a dent in the Vengal forces. People were dying in the streets at the hands of the ground troops while only a few starships had been destroyed. I decided to try something risky. I teleported down to the surface while

Gregorical hid among the towers of the city. My plan was to negotiate a peace with the Vengals to save lives while reinforcements arrived. The Vengals had no interest in talking, however, and they took aim at me with their cannons. They struck me with a blast. I fell, and I was certain I would die."

The children were literally on the edge of their seats.

"As I laid there on my back with one of the Vengal warriors standing over me and ready to strike the deathblow, I looked toward the sky and saw one of the Vengal ships straying from the others. It opened fire on the ground troops and chased them away from my location. Miraculously, I was safe, but how I wondered." Darbian's eyes peered down. "Soon the light of the star was dimmed from my view and standing over me was Aculpus Atronis, one of the most highly regarded Wardein of our age. He took me by the hand and lifted me up. We transported aboard his ship and there he tended to my wounds. He showed me how he was able to commandeer one of the Vengal ships. He discovered a weakness in their software, hacked the most powerful ship in the group, and used it to knock the others out of the sky from behind. They never saw it coming. When that was done, he used it to fire on the Vengal ground troops and defeat them."

"That was brilliant," said Micah.

"Aculpus Atronis saved my life that day. More than that, he saved an entire planet from being conquered by oppressors. I owe him my life and good people throughout the universe owe him their freedom, for he has fought many wicked villains over the years, not just that day." Darbian paused. "I won't entertain the notion that Aculpus would ever turn to the ranks of evil."

Soon the planet of Crystal Dawn appeared in view. The planet was like a jewel in the sand. It had bright blue skies on the light side of the planet and deep blue on the dimmer side. There was no such thing as night on the planet Crystal Dawn. It was close enough to the center of the galaxy to be rid of true darkness.

As Gregorical approached, Stellar City shone from the surface like a beacon on the Northern hemisphere of the planet. The city took up a quarter of the surface and was laid out in the pattern of a starburst, thus the origin of the name.

Darbian placed his hand on the control panel and sent a message to the planet below. "This is Darbian of the Wardein aboard the sentient ship Gregorical. I am requesting an emergency meeting with the Council on the whereabouts of the Wardein and an imminent threat facing our peace. Please respond." Darbian removed his hand and waited.

They received back mostly static. The words were muffled, but they could make out one phrase. "There's a traitor in our midst!"

Darbian froze.

Gregorical broke the silence. "Sir, what action do we take?"

Darbian looked at the children and glared down at the planet. "Gregorical, get closer so I can teleport down. I have to meet the Council alone."

CHAPTER 11

GREGORICAL SHOT through the atmosphere of Crystal Dawn and surveyed Stellar City. "Sir, it appears the city has sustained significant damage."

"They've already been here," Darbian said under his breath.

Micah wrung his hands. "What do we do, Darbian?"

Darbian whipped himself up out of his captain's chair. "Gregorical, do you detect any vessels in the area? Anything that might not be Council friendly?"

"No, sir. The system appears to be clear of vessels," Gregorical replied.

"What do you mean? No vessels? There should be cleanup crews, Council guards, traders...there has to be someone moving through this system after what's happened." Darbian stared at the view of Stellar City from above.

"Analysis of the surface would suggest they attacked from orbit," Gregorical said.

"All that damage from orbit? What sort of machines could do that?" Darbian rubbed his jaw. "Is anyone left?"

Hannelore spoke up. "Darbian! Who sent that signal?"

Darbian looked around. "Who indeed? Gregorical, tele-port me down to the surface. I want you to place me outside the Grand Hall of the Council."

"Yes, sir," Gregorical replied.

"Children, you'll stay here. I don't know what I'm walking into and I will not put you in danger." Darbian nodded.

"When are you coming back?" asked Hannelore.

Darbian paused for a moment. "Soon my child."

"Sir, I detect faint life on the planet, however, I do not believe there are many people below," Gregorical said.

Darbian's eyes glazed over. "Gregorical, I want you to keep a constant scan on this system. If Halinkoy's ships return then take the children to safety, assuming you can still find it."

"You want us to leave you?" Micah grumbled.

"Yes, if they return, then you won't have time to come back and get me. If those ships can bring so much carnage to Crystal Dawn, then there's no telling what they could do to Gregorical if given a clean shot." Darbian offered a salute. "Don't worry about me, I'll manage."

Gregorical flew closer to the planet's surface. "I'll monitor your progress."

"From a safe distance," replied Darbian.

"Of course." Gregorical engaged the teleporter.

Darbian disappeared, and the children were left alone aboard Gregorical.

"What can we do, Gregorical? How can we help?" asked Hannelore.

"Best to stay out of the way for now," Gregorical replied as he flew back up into orbit.

* * *

Darbian appeared on the planet's surface outside the Grand Hall of the Council, a massive glass structure that now featured a few holes in its otherwise elegant design. He walked inside the Hall and called for survivors.

"Is anyone here?" Darbian shouted. "This is Darbian of the Wardein! Who responded to my message?"

A faint voice echoed through the chamber. "For your own sake, you shouldn't be here, but I'm glad someone came."

Darbian looked up and around. "Who's there?"

"Have you forgotten the voice of the Council? So soon?" spoke the voice.

"Show yourself," said Darbian.

"I am Erevosa, Acting Chief of the Council," said the voice. A woman walked out from behind a fallen rafter. She was dressed in a shining, bright blue gown as was the custom of the Council members. Her hands folded in front of her and although she had just endured an incredible trauma, she appeared to be at peace. She was humanoid, a member of the Grentchis race. One significant difference between humans and the Grentchis was the deep yellow skin. She was enchanting and graceful yet her yellowness might remind one of a sickness rather than a flower.

"The Chief of the Council is Xanabir. Where is he?" Darbian retorted.

"Xanabir was the first killed. I'm all that's left of the Council. I'm afraid you must deal with me," Erevosa replied.

"And why did they leave you alive?" Darbian asked.

"They didn't. Those who survived are still alive because

Halinkoy left to spring a trap. Fortune spared us in a manner of speaking." Erevosa stood stoic.

"You speak of traps. So you're the traitor?" Darbian lifted his arm and pointed it at Erevosa. He altered the setting to transform the stun weapon on his wrist into a deadly blaster instead.

"If I were the traitor, then I wouldn't have told you about the trap, now would I?" Erevosa replied. "The trap is to corner the last Council member and the last Warden together and to kill them in one symbolic show of strength and brashness."

"The last Warden? I'm not the last Warden. Aculpus Atronis survives." Darbian said as he pursed his lips.

"By now, you know who the traitor is, Darbian. Aculpus has betrayed us all. Why? I don't know, but he's a part of the trap, not a survivor of it. You're the last Warden, the last one sworn to protect this universe from the forces of evil," Erevosa said.

Darbian squinted, looked around the room, and asked. "If that were true then why didn't Aculpus kill me when he had the chance?"

"Because Halinkoy wanted to kill us in person rather than having a henchman do it. His arrogance knows no bounds. He'll be back soon if he isn't already. You're all that's left. The universe depends on you. All those who remain alive depend on you. And that's why I haven't attempted to flee. You must know the Secret of the Council," Erevosa said.

Gregorical's voice piped in over the communicator that Darbian carried with him. "Sir, several ships have just appeared above the surface of the planet. I believe they are hostile."

Darbian wailed, but spoke back. "How did they get here so fast? Why didn't you detect them earlier?"

"It appears they have a Wormhole Matrix. They entered the system undetected. Reckless, but they were able to calculate the precise position of the planet from a great distance." Gregorical responded.

"Where did they get that technology? Only the Wardein have ships that ability!" Darbian clenched his fist.

"It's clear now, isn't it Darbian? Aculpus has betrayed us and aided our enemy from within. He's even given them Wardein technology," Erevosa said.

A rumble came overhead. It was the sound of a ship descending, heading for the remains of the Grand Hall.

"It makes sense now," Darbian said. "Why Aculpus didn't follow us...why he was waiting for us at the Wardein base...why he was cloaked...why he survived at all to tell the tale. There's only one explanation. A Warden has never turned before. Not until now."

"I'm sorry, Darbian, but that's the least of our worries. Halinkoy has returned. You can hear his ship overhead," Erevosa said.

"He was my mentor. He was everyone's friend. Why would he do this? How many people have died because of his treachery?" Darbian buried his face in his hands.

"You must leave now, Darbian, and take the Secret with you," Erevosa said.

Darbian reached for his communicator. "Gregorical, it's too late. Take the children and head for safety. Get as far away from this planet as you can. You're their watchman now. Take good care of them. You're all they have left."

"Sir, there's still time to teleport you and the Council Chief away from the surface." Gregorical begged.

"No, my friend," said Darbian. "I'll stay here. I'll face

Halinkoy myself and put an end to this nightmare once and for all. Either that or I'll die trying."

Erevosa approached Darbian. "Darbian, you must leave this planet at once before Halinkoy arrives. You won't survive his wrath. I'll remain. I'll be the bait. You must live. There's no battle to be won here."

"I have to face him," Darbian said.

"You must preserve the Secret, Darbian." Erevosa opened her arms and peered around the room. "No one else is left."

The sound of a battleship echoed in the sky overhead. Death was coming. Halinkoy had arrived and there was no time to make a plan, no time to decide. Instinct would prevail.

"I'll go then. Tell me the secret," said Darbian.

"No, not something to be told. It's something to be protected. It is a thing, not a word." Erevosa reached into her pocket and pulled out a disc. "This will grant you access to the Astrolabe."

"The what?" Darbian flailed his arms.

The rumble in the sky grew deeper and louder. A shadow shrouded the whole structure.

"No time for talk. Are you listening, Darbian? It all depends on you. You have one chance. One chance to know the Secret. One chance to memorize the coordinates of the Astrolabe. I'll be dead soon and the whereabouts will be lost to history unless you do your duty. Proceed to Alpha Kappa 102457739 Omicron 488. There you'll find the Astrolabe. There you'll find the Secret." Erevosa handed the disc to Darbian.

Darbian took it with his hand shaking. "Say the coordinates one more time before he arrives."

The Grand Hall rattled.

"No time. He's here," said Erevosa.

What was left of the roof exploded from the force of Halinkoy's ship plunging itself into the building.

Erevosa and Darbian were blown backwards several meters while rock, glass, and metal were strewn all over the floor.

Halinkoy's ship came to rest inside the Grand Hall. It was a silvery, saucer-like craft.

The door was oval-shaped, and it opened soon after the arrival. A ramp stretched down to the floor of the Hall. Smoke emanated from the entrance while a bright, pulsating light shone out of the doorway and permeated the wrecked edifice.

Erevosa laid on the ground, but pulled herself up. "Run, Darbian. No more time."

The blast stunned Darbian, and he was slow to get up.

Suddenly, a shadow blocked the light and a blight on the universe made its appearance.

The sound of clanking footsteps filled the room. Out of the doorway came a thing, a massive robotic form. It walked down the ramp and clanked with each step. It stood twice as tall as a normal person and featured laser cannons on either arm. A globe, a device made to give the creature a 360-degree view and yet allow its head to remain protected, topped its shoulders. Every inch of the mechanized creature was covered in armor but it bore no markings.

Erevosa stood up, raised her head toward the mechanized monster, and spoke. "Your doom is upon you."

A voice like thunder grumbled and hawed. "Erevosa," came from the thing and it sounded as though it were the voice of darkness itself. "Your doom is upon you!" With that, he stretched out his arm and fired his laser cannon.

The laser blast hit Erevosa, and she fell to the ground.

"Long live the Timekeeper," she said as a burning plasma consumed most of her body.

The mechanized form turned his gaze a few meters away toward Darbian. "What is your name, Warden?"

Darbian lifted himself to his knees. "My name is Darbian, Warden of Sector 401."

"No, you're the only Warden! It doesn't matter what Sector you came from," the mechanized form said. "I like you on your knees, Warden. It befits a slave. Stay there and prepare to worship me. I'm your new king after all."

Darbian placed his hand on the floor and it appeared as though he bowed. His knees were weak and his expression had fallen. His fingers trembled under the weight of his body, but he pressed down and pushed himself up from the ground. He stood. "I worship no man."

"Ajax Halinkoy is no mere man," the form said.

Darbian lifted his arm and prepared to fire his weapon. "Gregorical, can you hear me? I think there's a sufficient hole in the roof now that you can teleport me out. Come quickly," Darbian whispered.

"That puny blaster?" Halinkoy laughed.

Gregorical sent back a sequence of beeping sounds over the communicator.

It was two beeps and one short blip. This was a coded message as Gregorical understood that a vocal response would expose their plan to the enemy. The signal indicated that the teleportation device wasn't working.

Darbian fired and the energy of the blast was scattered all over Halinkoy's mechanized suit. Darbian fired again and again with the same result.

Halinkoy continued walking towards Darbian. "Warden, you amuse me. Perhaps I'll let you live for a while longer." He reached out for Darbian's throat, grabbed him, and lifted him off the ground.

Darbian struggled, fired his blaster several more times, but could barely breathe. With a muffled voice, he spoke, "Halinkoy, I'll never bow to the likes of you. Kill me if you wish."

"By the way, I'm now familiar with your coded messaging system. Your old friend Aculpus gave us that information. If you're wondering why your teleportation device isn't working, it's because I'm not stupid enough to think you arrived on this planet without a ship! The entire system is being flooded with a certain energy signature. It interferes with teleporters and I'm afraid you won't be going anywhere." Halinkoy squeezed Darbian's throat.

"Death it is then," said Darbian.

"No, no, Warden. I don't want to kill you yet. I want you to suffer. After I've had my fun with you, well, then I'll kill you." Halinkoy dropped Darbian to the ground.

At that moment, several soldiers marched out of Halinkoy's craft. They were of a race familiar to Darbian, at least in appearance.

"Do you recognize their form, Warden? You've never seen them in the flesh, but I know you've seen images. They're Tammeder soldiers. Yes, they've returned from a long slumber to accomplish what they set out to do millions of years ago, to conquer this universe and rid it of self-righteous do-gooders such as yourself." Halinkoy laughed. "Tie him up and prepare the broadcast. It's time to show everyone that today is a holiday. Today is the day the Wardein are defeated once and for all."

The Tammeder soldiers brought chains and tied up Darbian to one of the remaining pillars in the Grand Hall.

"I failed you, Erevosa," said Darbian.

CHAPTER 12

THREE LARGE BATTLESHIPS had positioned themselves in orbit over Crystal Dawn. These were Halinkoy's flagships and the most powerful in his fleet.

Millions of miles away, however, Gregorical had hidden himself behind one of Crystal Dawn's moons. He followed Darbian's instructions only so far as to remove himself from detection.

Micah fell to the floor and cried. "What are we going to do, Gregorical?"

Gregorical had monitored the exchange on the planet. He and the children heard everything.

Hannelore stared at the main screen and watched Halinkoy's battleships. "What if we go down to the planet and rescue Darbian?"

Gregorical found himself in the role of the children's guardian. "No, my children, putting you in harm's way is not an option. I will protect you as Darbian commanded me to. We will find a safe place."

Micah stopped crying long enough to ask, "Is there a safe place now with the Wardein gone?"

Gregorical's tone of voice changed for the first time in front of the children. A worried sound from a being with no real emotions was quite an unusual thing to hear.

"Young one, that's hard to answer, but I have a duty to see you to safety. I'll return you to your home planet and stand guard above it. It's unlikely that Halinkoy will seek to rule every planet directly, especially one whose people lack the ability to traverse the stars," Gregorical said.

"We can't leave Darbian here. He'll die," said Hannelore.

Gregorical didn't wish to scare the children, but he realized they were naive. "Children, if I do not take you away from here, you may die as well."

Hannelore walked to her chair and slunk over the back. "Then why haven't we already left, Gregorical? What are we still doing here?"

"Hope," responded Gregorical. "I suppose I still have some left."

* * *

"Oh, Darbian, you're privileged. You're the first outsider who will hear the story of how this universe came to be conquered." Halinkoy paced back and forth across the room.

Meanwhile, the Tammeder soldiers scurried about the room. This was no illusion or grand deception. Each one was a genuine member of the ancient Tammeder Clan. They were green, scaly creatures. It would be incorrect to label them as reptiles, however, as reptiles were native to Earth. The Tammeder were tall and strong. They each wore armor that exposed their muscles but protected their vital and most vulnerable parts. Focused and unrelenting in their goals, they didn't pay much attention to the world around them. There was a deadness in their eyes, however. The Tammeder weren't known to enjoy anything.

"Did you know, Darbian, that the Tammeder saved me?" Halinkoy looked into Darbian's eyes.

Darbian's mouth opened. There was a question on his lips, but he wasn't sure how to ask.

"Oh yes. They saved me from a meaningless existence." Halinkoy turned his back. "I'm from Earth, you know. I suppose you've already guessed that."

Darbian flared his nose. "I had an inkling you might be."

"But what you don't know is how I came to be their master. They saved me, yes, and then I returned the favor. They were lost, and I gave them purpose. After their defeat at the hands of the Wardein, they needed a reason to go on. Revenge would have been a great motivator, no doubt, but most of their brethren were dead and even their supreme leader was killed in battle. They needed a new leader, and I needed followers." Halinkoy remained with his back to Darbian.

"Followers? Why would they follow you?" Darbian asked.

Halinkoy laughed. "How stupid you are, Warden. They follow me because I'm a god in the making."

Darbian tried to respond, but couldn't muster up any words.

"Yes, that's right." Halinkoy turned around and stared at Darbian. He opened his globe helmet and revealed his face, a steel-blue-eyed man with blonde hair. He had a face that wasn't at all unusual, a gaze that wasn't at all haunting for such a villainous man. Now, his voice sounded like that of a normal human. He was a calm speaker. "I'm human for now, but soon a god. This universe and its peoples will bend to my will. Everyone who stands in my way will be destroyed."

"What gives you the right to proclaim yourself a god?" Darbian fired back.

Halinkoy twitched his eye. "What right do I need? It's what needs to be done." He closed his globe helmet once more.

"That's no reason. That's a maniacal ambition," Darbian said.

"It's not maniacal. It's destiny. I may be from Earth, but that pale blue dot was always too small for me. It was never enough. Those pathetic people who occupy that planet, they were never worthy of my presence." Halinkoy walked around once more. "As pointless as that little blue rock is, that's precisely where the Tammeder ended up after their odyssey."

"How is that possible?" Darbian asked.

"Oh yes, you've always been taught that the Tammeder simply disappeared. That they were in the midst of battle and vanished into nothingness." Halinkoy laughed again. "How stupid can you be? You never even imagined that their technology was far beyond that of your own. You never took the time to ask why, not the slightest spark of curiosity. That's why you're not worthy, Warden. No ability to see anything other than what's right in front of your face."

Darbian hung his head as he understood there was truth to what Halinkoy was saying.

"The Tammeder didn't disappear. They fled to fight another day. They engaged their greatest technology, a hyperspace drive that would instantly fling them to another part of the universe in the event of an emergency. Their craft, damaged and weakened by the immense energy needed to make such a journey, crashed on a rocky, barren Earth. Repairing their ship was impossible in that environment. They were stranded. There was no civilization to speak of, no energy source to tap. So they hibernated until they could find a more suitable energy source. They would wait and build a new world. Something went wrong though. Their hibernation chambers never woke them up. They slept for three million years until one fateful day." Halinkoy called out to one of his soldiers. "Is the equipment almost ready? I tire of this Warden. He's too stupid for an interesting conversation."

"What fateful day?" asked Darbian.

"The day I discovered them." Halinkoy walked over to a control panel set up by the Tammeder and investigated their work. "I'm a scientist by trade, Warden. I have a background in a variety of disciplines: geology, theoretical physics, aerospace engineering, and even botany."

Darbian sneered. "Well, that's magnificent."

"You should be impressed," responded Halinkoy. "I am, by far, the smartest human ever to live. You should be honored to meet me."

"I already told you I was," Darbian said. "But I'd be more impressed if you told me how the Tammeder came to follow you."

"I suppose you would," said Halinkoy. "I should start from the beginning, however. Besides being the planet's top scientist, I was interested in making the world a better place. Why not, eh? If I had to be stuck on that forsaken rock then I suppose I should be concerned about its well-being. So I attempted to draw people to my cause, people who could understand the human race was underachieving and, therefore, should have their ways altered. Some followed me. Others called me a false messiah."

"What you're saying is you founded a cult?" Darbian looked up.

"A cult? Ha! So cynical you are, devoid of vision. It's no wonder your corps has perished. No imagination. You think you understand how the universe works. You think the order of things is something to be examined and accepted. I suppose nothing escapes your gaze as long as someone hands it to you on a platter." Halinkoy continued to investigate the control panel.

"What would you call it?" Darbian asked.

"A society of the enlightened and the wise. We built a community in England at first. After a few years, their government persecuted us and chased us out of the country. We went to South America and eventually the same thing happened. Then to an island in the South Pacific where we finally had some peace, some opportunity to work on our endeavors. But fate had us there for a purpose. Yes, and it wasn't to make the discoveries that would save Earth. No, it was there we found the power to destroy." Halinkoy put his hands together and squeezed.

"What does that mean?" Darbian's ears perked up.

"It means that once our plans are cemented, we'll return to Earth and annihilate it. Just as we annihilated the Wardein. Just as we'll annihilate this planet and any other that impedes our family realizing our potential. The universe cannot survive without our intervention, Darbian. You can't see that by now? The wars, the villains, the natural disasters, all the utter chaos. The order of the universe is not to be accepted as it is." Halinkoy pounded his fist on the panel in front of him. "We must remake the order, an order that suits us best."

Darbian shuddered. "How does destroying anyone prevent war and chaos?"

Halinkoy approached Darbian again and pulled Darbian's head back by his hair. "We destroy the unworthy. Haven't you been listening?"

"And you get to decide who's worthy and who isn't?" Darbian said as he was being manhandled.

"Of course, I decide. The universe chose me...it granted me the power to decide. So why not me?" Halinkoy threw Darbian's head against the column and then released him.

Darbian shook his head. "Tell me, Halinkoy. Why Earth? Why would you destroy a planet like that? They can't stop you."

"They had their chance, and they didn't follow me. That tiny little world...they could have been so much more, but they chose insignificance and I'll grant it to them. Earth is a meaningless world, and I outgrew it a long time ago. Don't worry, Darbian. I'll see that your death precedes that of Earth if you care for it. Compassion is important, you know." Halinkoy turned his back again.

* * *

"They're going to destroy Earth," said Hannelore.

"There is no safe place, Gregorical. Not Earth," said Micah

"We'll have to find another planet. Fortunately, there are many suitable planets in the universe," Gregorical stated as he plotted a course for a planet far away from Halinkoy.

"We can't go into hiding, Gregorical. What about our families? What about Earth?" Micah breathed heavily.

"And what about Darbian?" cried Hannelore.

"I am under orders from Darbian, my children. It would be inappropriate to disobey my commanding officer," Gregorical said with a hint of sadness in his voice.

Micah hit the control panel with both fists. "What about that hope? You said you still had hope."

"Darbian wouldn't leave us. That's for sure!" Hannelore said as she tried to hold back tears.

"We have to do something. No one is safe." Micah spun around. "It's the Star Force creed. 'Have Courage, Have Strength, Protect the Innocent,'" he said.

Gregorical interjected. "Children...please."

"Darbian saved us! Now, we have to be there to save him. We have to try." Micah looked up at the ceiling as he was in the habit of doing when he wanted to speak to Gregorical. "We have to at least try! Gregorical, please."

Gregorical brought up a schematic of the Grand Hall on his main screen. "Children...if we are to try, then we must have a plan. We must have the element of surprise. We are one ship against an army."

* * *

"You said it needed to be done," said Darbian as he stared at the floor. "You want to be a god because it needs to be done? That doesn't make any sense."

"I'm sure it doesn't make sense to you. You've probably never experienced anything but tranquility in your time, a superb and comfortable life I imagine," Halinkoy said.

"You imagine wrong then," replied Darbian.

Halinkoy approached Darbian once again. "Tell me Warden, what sort of chaos have you seen?"

"Other than my brethren being taken from this universe? Where would you like me to begin?" Darbian said.

Halinkoy laughed. "You should thank me for that. It was the first step in protecting this universe from itself."

"You didn't answer the question," Darbian glared back up.

"Isn't it obvious to you Warden? The universe needs a master. Oh sure, some believe in other realms and some higher power, but it's all a fairy tale." Halinkoy folded his arms behind his back.

"You think the universe needs a master? Seems to be running fine on its own," said Darbian.

"Really now? Then why did the Council create the Wardein? Because the universe was running just fine on its own? You're not that stupid," Halinkoy replied.

Darbian leered to his side. "I thought you believed the Wardein were part of the problem?"

"I never said that, Warden. Your order was weak. That's what I said. The Wardein were wholly incapable of managing all the terrors that the universe could throw at them," Halinkoy said.

Darbian pursed his lips. "Then why destroy us?"

"There can only be one master, Warden. Only one can rule and it should naturally be the most worthy," Halinkoy replied.

Darbian raised his eyebrow. "You're a piece of work."

Halinkoy slapped Darbian, nearly knocking him unconscious. "Where were you when my family was taken from me? Where were any of you?"

Darbian sniffed and took a deep breath to regain his composure.

"Heroes? Hardly." Halinkoy kicked a fallen stone and launched it into what remained of the wall.

Darbian refocused. "What happened to you?"

"What happened to me?" Halinkoy paused. "I was just a boy. My parents were killed in a hurricane. An act of God they called it. Only a cruel God would act in such a way, but I soon discovered there was no such being. There was no one to comfort me, no one to protect me when my parents were gone. I was all alone. I shifted from home to home, foster care they called it...another miserable invention of the humans. If it weren't for my brilliance, I would have fallen by the wayside. Eventually, I made a life for myself and rose above my circumstances. It took time, but I made peace with it all. I came to understand that Mother Nature is harsh, but at least she's fair."

"I'm sorry that happened to you," replied Darbian.

"And that's the answer to your question Warden. Why must I become a god? There's no one else to do it." Halinkoy plodded off.

* * *

Gregorical searched his databanks for strategies on dealing with insurmountable odds. Despite great trouble in finding a similar situation, he came across an example.

"So you've got a plan, right?" Micah said as he slapped his hands together.

"It's reckless, frankly, but I found something that might work." Gregorical brought up a file on his main screen.

"So we'll need a little luck is what you're saying?" Hannelore replied.

"Luck is an imaginary construct my child. There's no such thing," Gregorical didn't quite have the capacity to relate to humans. He had only recently met humans for the first time, however, so there was no point in blaming him.

"My Irish granddad would beg to differ," Hannelore retorted.

Gregorical continued. "On screen now is a diagram of a sneak attack by two Wardein many centuries ago. It involved worm holing into a building from the orbit of the planet. It's even more reckless than the Tammeder ships worm holing into orbit from a great distance. If I make the wrong move, then we'll all be vaporized."

"I wonder if that would be painful?" Hannelore offered.

"Exceedingly," replied Gregorical.

Micah pointed to the schematic of the Grand Hall. "But it might work, right?"

"It might work, my child," said Gregorical.

"So we wormhole in and, Gregorical, you shoot the soldiers with your lasers? That sounds easy," Hannelore shrugged her shoulders.

"No, it's not that easy. My lasers are made from the same technology that powers Darbian's wrist weapon. His laser was completely ineffective against Halinkoy's suit and I estimate that the likelihood of the Tammeder armor being made of the same material is 93.5%. We must come up with something else," said Gregorical.

"What if we ram him?" Micah grabbed Hannelore's shoulder.

Hannelore's face brightened. "Right, we could knock him over like bowling pins."

"I'm afraid not. It is unknown what material Halinkoy's armor is made of. It's possible he could crack my hull," replied Gregorical.

Hannelore placed her hands over her cheeks. "What if we knock the building down on top of him? That would at least slow him down."

Gregorical's tone soured. "And Darbian would likely not survive that, my dear."

Within an instant, an alarm rang out inside the ship. The sound pierced the children's ears. Red lights were flashing and from the ceiling sprung weapons on robotic arms.

"A temporal displacement has been detected. An intruder is aboard the ship," Gregorical said.

A new schematic appeared on the main screen, this one a chart of Gregorical's interior.

A blinking red dot showed where the intruder was located.

Whoever it was had penetrated the docking bay.

"What?" shouted Micah.

"That's all we need!" said Hannelore

"It's logical to conclude the ship has been boarded by a time traveler," replied Gregorical. "Children, for your safety, please follow the glowing red arrows to a secure room at the heart of the ship. I will try to vacate our intruder using extreme tactics."

The children followed the arrows. They ran down the hall as fast as the sharp corners would allow them.

Just as Micah made the last turn to approach the safe room, he caught something peculiar out of the corner of his eye. "It's a Warden."

"It's a what?" replied Hannelore.

"I saw a Warden. He moved around the corner as soon as I saw him." Micah stopped and stared down the hallway. "I think we need to follow him."

"Are you crazy? What if it's Aculpus? He's the only other Warden out there! What if he's followed us to finish us off?" Hannelore's knees knocked together.

"No," Micah whispered. "He doesn't want to hurt us. Aculpus would chase us. It's almost like this one is hiding from us." Micah turned away from the red arrows and followed the mystery figure.

"Children, I must insist that you return to the safe

room. I do not know the identity of the intruder," Gregorical said.

Hannelore jetted after Micah. "I get in more trouble following you around."

Micah chased the figure around a few corners before the person he saw disappeared behind a wall.

An alarm rang out once again.

"Temporal displacement detected. The intruder appears to have left the ship," said Gregorical.

Micah slowed down and walked around the wall where he last saw the mystery figure. He spied an object on the ground. "What's this?"

"What's what?" replied Hannelore.

Micah stooped down to get a closer look at what appeared to be a large gun lying on the floor.

Hannelore tried to pull Micah back. "Don't touch it Micah! Why can't boys be both brave and smart at the same time?"

"Wait, wait!" Micah said. "I think he left it for us."

CHAPTER 13

DARBIAN LOOKED UP AT HALINKOY. "You never told me the rest of the story. How did you meet the Tammeder? What would make them follow you?"

"On the island that was our home, we made a habit of excavating in the caverns. We searched for precious metals and minerals to trade with the outside world. We needed various supplies to conduct our research...instruments, chemicals. But one day...the day destiny found me...we discovered something altogether spectacular." Halinkoy looked at his soldiers with pride. "We found the door to a spaceship."

"The Tammeder," said Darbian.

"Of course. We found hundreds of pods with alien beings inside. They were alive, and we understood it to be a form of hibernation. Suddenly, the pods opened. The Tammeder came to life. But, they were quite upset that strangers had intruded upon their ship. They killed most of our excavation team. Then they came to me. They looked into my eyes and their anger left. Their fierceness turned to calm." Halinkoy let out a sigh of relief.

Darbian's eyes narrowed. "Why would they spare you?"

"They saw in me the spirit of a leader." Halinkoy raised his hands up to the sky. "They saw their future. At some point in the past, a prophet of the Tammeder saw the influence I could have. He embedded my image and name in the mind of every Tammeder being. Once they knew who I was, they followed me readily."

"You didn't care they had murdered your friends?" Darbian blurted.

"Of course not. Sometimes sacrifices are necessary." Halinkoy said. "What was important is that they served their purpose and that they would allow me to serve mine. The Tammeder had a rightful heir to their legacy and at that moment, we were all put on this course. Even you Warden."

"What do you mean?" Darbian tilted his head.

Halinkoy's shining dome edged closer to Darbian's face. "Haven't you wondered why you survived? Haven't you asked yourself the question?"

"You're talking about the Time Bomb," replied Darbian.

"The last Warden, the only one left standing. How is that possible? Why weren't you with the others when they met their demise?" Halinkoy gripped the chains holding down Darbian and rattled them.

"I was away doing my duty. What sort of question is that?" Darbian bristled.

"You've been my prisoner for far longer than you realize, Warden." Halinkoy gripped Darbian's chin. "I let you live."

Darbian fell silent.

"When I procured the services of Aculpus Atronis, I asked him who the most incapable Warden was. I said to him 'Tell me Aculpus, who is the weakest link?'" Halinkoy let go of Darbian's chin. "It was you."

Darbian would have fought such an accusation, but there he stood bound in chains and helpless. His greatest fear was realized. He was too weak to save himself much less anyone else.

"I sent Vinitor to Earth, and I made sure you heard a call for help...to lure you out and keep you busy. That's why you're here. It's not because you were wise or brave. You didn't escape destruction even by luck. You are here because you are weak." Halinkoy turned his back. "You're a symbol, Warden. You represent just how useless and inadequate the institution of the Wardein is. I told you earlier that I don't want to kill you yet. Why do you think that is?"

"You said you wanted me to suffer," Darbian replied.

"Oh, but it's so much deeper than that," said Halinkoy. "I want to parade the last Warden around this universe and prove to everyone...every living thing...that your kind is weak and that I'm supreme. If you were dead, they would only see your corpse, but I want them to see your shattered soul and know their hope is dead."

Darbian hung his head.

"And when I've proven just how fragile your order is... just how feeble your efforts are...then I'll put you out of your misery, but not a moment sooner." Halinkoy said.

Darbian grew angry. "Maybe you're the weak one."

Halinkoy laughed.

"Is it funny? Wouldn't you want to make a show of the strongest Warden? But you weren't capable of that, were you?" Darbian gritted his teeth.

"Strongest Warden? The strong know when they've been bested. The strong would submit." Halinkoy turned back to face Darbian. "Oh yes, in fact, that is exactly what happened. Aculpus joined me because he was the strongest, the only one worthy of my vision. It's the weak that resist the inevitable."

"There's nothing inevitable about you," Darbian replied.

"What's inevitable is that all will worship me or die." Halinkoy said. "Which brings me to Crystal Dawn...literally."

"You want to send a message?" Darbian replied.

"Precisely. I've come to the home of the Council, the only place in the universe that has the technology capable of broadcasting a message to every planet in existence. It's only fitting I should stand here in the ruins of the Council to tell the cosmos of their fate." Halinkoy thrust his hands upward. "What's taking so long?"

"Only a moment more, my Supreme One," said one of the Tammeder soldiers.

Halinkoy grumbled. "Unfortunately, our first attack was a little too thorough and damaged some equipment. The Tammeder are fine technicians, but a little slow."

"I suppose that's what you get when you break things," Darbian sneered.

Halinkoy paced. "The entire universe needs to understand what you have now seen, Warden, that a new day is about to dawn. Midnight is coming."

"How would you conquer an entire universe? It's not possible," Darbian replied.

"The Tammeder have been replenished. Their finest soldiers have been cloned over and over again. I have quadrillions at my disposal," Halinkoy said. "The ships in orbit? A mere drop in the bucket compared to the forces I have."

"The others? The other members of your society, what happened to them?" Darbian probed Halinkoy.

"Still worried about the broken eggs, eh?" Halinkoy paused. He peered toward the floor. "I suppose I can tell you. It's not as though you'll survive long enough to do anything about it."

"What's that?" Darbian asked.

"One of the technologies we found on the Tammeder craft allowed me to amplify my intelligence." Halinkoy said. "I had my subjects immersed in a mind-numbing stasis so their intelligence, their literal consciousness could be transmitted to my mind and enhance its abilities. My human followers were more than willing to sacrifice themselves so I could be everything I was to be."

Darbian's look grew hollow. "So they're dead?"

Halinkoy moaned. "Not at all. They live on in stasis along with some of the great minds of history."

"Great minds of history?" Darbian said.

Halinkoy called to one of his soldiers. "Bring down my throne. I'm ready to sit and present myself to my empire."

Some Tammeder soldiers brought down Halinkoy's throne from his ship. It was made of gold with spires emerging from nine points.

Halinkoy sat down. "As my intelligence increased, so did my ambition. That's when I made my ascension a sure thing."

"Yes, you're full of ambition, aren't you?" Darbian recoiled.

"Why shouldn't I be? Who else could hack the greatest technologies ever created by the greatest warrior race that ever existed?" Halinkoy tapped the arm of his throne. "Not only did I use their technology to enhance my intelligence, I altered their hyper-drive device to create time travel from scratch! I journeyed to numerous points throughout human history and captured some of humanity's most intelligent. They weren't willing to be my puppets, but that made no difference. We forced them into stasis and I enjoy their minds every moment.

"This technology will only work with people of the same species, I presume?" Darbian asserted.

"Oh, quite clever, Warden. It's the first intelligent thing you've said today." Halinkoy laughed.

"You said their consciousness was being broadcast into your mind. All those people inside your head. Surely there's something left of them. There are good people inside your mind. Doesn't that bother you?" Darbian asked with a sly grin.

Halinkoy sighed and ignored the question.

* * *

Back aboard Gregorical, the children were confused by the device laying at their feet.

"Children," said Gregorical. "It would be advisable if you heeded my warnings in the future. There are many dangers in outer space you are not familiar with. Time travel is one of them."

"He didn't want to hurt us though, Gregorical. He never even tried to attack us," Micah replied.

"Whoever this person was and whatever he left behind are very dangerous, nonetheless. You should have listened." Gregorical turned off the red arrows.

"It looks like a weapon," said Hannelore.

The device was a long metal tube with four handles on either side placed at equal distances. The trigger was the size of a human hand and protruded from the bottom. It shined like chrome except for a black bit of rubber lining that protected the muzzle end.

"Gregorical, you said he was a time traveler. What if he was here to help us? What if he couldn't tell us who he was?" Micah took a step closer to the device.

"Before you touch it, let me analyze it first." Gregorical deployed a node from the ceiling that scanned the device.

"What is it?" Hannelore said.

"It is indeed a weapon. The internal mechanisms were fashioned by Nexarum scientists, but the design is unknown." Gregorical retracted the node back into the ceiling.

"What does that mean?" Micah looked at the ceiling.

"It's from the future. The design is not on file so that is the only reasonable conclusion," said Gregorical. "The device appears to contain mircobots capable of disintegrating various types of metallic structures via a process resembling digestion."

"It eats metal?" Hannelore cocked her head to the side.

"A Metal-Eater," said Micah.

Gregorical chimed in. "Simplistic, yet catchy."

"This can beat Halinkoy!" Micah pumped his fist.

"I assume you want to attack by deploying this weapon on Halinkoy's suit," Gregorical said.

"Exactly. We can use this to eat the suit up. That should distract them long enough for us to get away." Micah grinned as brightly and widely as he ever had.

Gregorical spoke. "I believe you'll both have to hold it up. It's quite heavy."

"We can do it, right Hannelore?" Micah pointed at his friend.

"I'll give it a try!" she said.

"The weapon is untested. There is no guarantee this

will work on any level." Gregorical then opened a door to the corridor that led to the bay door and turned on the yellow arrows to guide the children's way.

"You want us to try it though," said Hannelore.

"The plan, children, is to wormhole into the Grand Hall with Darbian and Halinkoy. I'll open the bay door from the rear and you'll only have a few seconds to fire the weapon. Take great care." Gregorical prepared the calculations to wormhole onto the planet and into the same room with Darbian. "Children, take the weapon and go to the back of the ship. Strap yourselves in. We're about to make ourselves known to the Tammeder ships."

"Yes, sir!" shouted Micah.

Hannelore struggled as she picked up her end of the weapon. "This better work."

The children hauled the device to the back of the ship and strapped themselves into a set of chairs just above the bay door.

"No more time to waste children. We're going." With that, Gregorical initiated the Chrono drive and formed a wormhole on just the other side of the moon they had been hiding behind.

* * *

Aboard the Tammeder flagship, its Captain noticed a wormhole forming on the starboard side. "Who is that?" he exclaimed.

At that moment, Gregorical emerged from the other side of the moon and flew into the wormhole.

"Alert the Supreme One!" screamed the Captain.

* * *

"The broadcast is ready to begin, Supreme One," stated one soldier.

"Good. I want the camera on me first. Be prepared to change the scenery at my direction," said Halinkoy.

The soldier nodded. "Yes, my Supreme One!

The broadcast began.

"Greetings to all intelligent races on the countless worlds of our shared universe. I bring you wonderful news. As of today, you have a new emperor...a new Supreme One." Halinkoy opened his arms.

Many peoples from across the universe were instantly made aware of the broadcast on their respective worlds, ships, and outposts. They felt compelled to watch the proceedings as this message interrupted their usual broadcasts. Governments, common people, soldiers, and pirates alike were taken aback at the feed as it was so very rare for someone to send a universe-wide message from Crystal Dawn at all.

Halinkoy stood up from his throne and approached the camera. "Your institutions have failed you. You've put all your hope and faith in miserable and weak leaders, but they couldn't protect you...not even from me. And so it's only proper I come to you today and tell you that a new order is being established. We are about to bring true peace after an eternity of war and destruction."

Peoples from all across the universe watched intently, but none understood what was happening.

"Soon, you'll worship me in the manner I deserve," Halinkoy continued. "But first, you must know why I deserve to be worshipped, why I'm worthy of your unquestioning allegiance."

The camera swung to Darbian in his beaten state, tied to a pillar in the Grand Hall.

"You see this man? He's the last of his kind. Who is he?" Halinkoy chuckled. "He's a Warden. Yes, that's right. The Wardein have been defeated, and here you see the great planet Crystal Dawn fallen to its knees!" Halinkoy's voice hit another octave. "The Council is dead. Here, on the planet where the Wardein were formed, their final representative is bruised and all but dead. It's true. Some of you are afraid now, and perhaps you should be."

Darbian said nothing. He simply looked at the ground.

Halinkoy continued. "My rule will be a compassionate one. For everyone who bends the knee, there will be great prosperity. But for those who defy me, there will be utter destruction. Choose wisely. For, I'll be touring each of your planets soon to make my reign secure. There I'll parade the last Warden for all to see and all will understand that your great heroes can no longer save you."

At that instant, inside the Grand Hall, a wormhole appeared. The force of it cracked what remaining glass there was in the building.

Gregorical emerged from the wormhole and stopped approximately two inches from Darbian's face.

"Sorry, sir. I cut that a bit closer than I intended," Gregorical's voice boomed out into the Hall.

Darbian's mouth hung open. "That's okay."

Gregorical swung around until the bow of the ship faced Halinkoy. The bay door opened as the Tammeder fired at the hull of the ship.

All of this was being caught on camera and broadcast live to a universe told to abandon hope.

As the bay door opened, the children popped out with the Metal-Eater in hand. Each child held up one side and Hannelore's hand was planted on the trigger.

"That pale blue dot? That's my home, and I happen to like it, you jerk-bucket!" Hannelore pulled the trigger.

The force of the weapon moved the muzzle up several inches upon firing. The recoil was enough to alter the aim and nearly send the children flying onto their backs.

From out of the Metal-Eater came a ball of something... a group of mircobots is what Gregorical would have called them. The ball bounced off the walls several times, catching the attention of the Tammeder soldiers along the way, before resting on Halinkoy's throne. From there, the ball disassembled itself into twelve robotic, spider-looking creatures that rotated around the object they had landed upon. They ate the metal as locusts would devour a crop. They reduced the throne to dust in a matter of seconds.

Halinkoy grimaced. "Micah?" he wondered aloud. His face was pained as though he had just been struck with a great headache.

"How do you know my name?" Micah nearly dropped the weapon.

"Never mind, we have to save Darbian," Hannelore implored.

"What was that?" shouted Darbian.

The metal eating robots scrambled in all directions. Some crawled onto the Tammeder soldiers and ate their armor. Others looked for a meal in the walls themselves or the implements of the Council found in the room.

In the confusion, the Tammeder soldiers fired at each other in an attempt to destroy the robotic creatures. This plan failed miserably as many Tammeder fell to friendly fire.

"Fire again!" shouted Darbian.

The children aimed for Halinkoy once again and fired. A similar recoil occurred, and this ball bounced off a few

Tammeder before coming to rest near the pillar where Darbian was tied up.

"Aim lower children! Aim lower!" Darbian cheered for his young friends.

The children took aim at the ground below Halinkoy.

The Metal-Eater beeped, and a computerized voice blurted out "one shot remaining."

"This one has to work!" Sweat dripped from Micah's forehead.

Hannelore stared at the Metal-Eater. "Now you tell me?"

Halinkoy tried to shake off the pain. "Fire at those children! Fire!" He now and took aim with his own weapon.

Hannelore pulled the trigger once more.

The final ball bounced off the ground in front of Halinkoy and ricocheted directly into his chest. It knocked him off his feet and into the pile of dust that used to be his throne.

The metal eating robots went to work once more chewing up Halinkoy's armored suit as he lay on the ground, helpless to stop them.

The children dropped the Metal-Eater, jumped down off the bay door, and ran for Darbian, hoping to free him from his shackles. They discovered, however, that the metal eating robots had already done most of the work for them.

Darbian fired his weapon at the remaining shackles and they fell off his body. He was still bruised and still beaten, but as resolved as ever to protect the children from any harm. He met them halfway across the room. "Back into the bay children!"

Gregorical whipped around to make it easier for Darbian and the children to get back on board as the

Tammeder soldiers finally realized what was happening and had taken aim at the Warden.

The children leapt back onto the ship with Darbian soon behind them.

As all were aboard the ship once again, Gregorical closed the bay door.

"Can you blast through the ceiling Gregorical?" Darbian asked as he sat in his chair for the first time in what seemed like days.

"No problem, sir. Not much of it left." Gregorical responded.

"Then get us out of here fast," Darbian said.

Gregorical engaged his Galacto drive and sped through the rest of the ceiling in the Grand Hall. Leaving the ruins behind, he sped away from the planet.

A screeching Halinkoy was helped to his feet by the remainder of his soldiers. They boarded their ship and as well and sped away from the planet back to their flagship.

What remained of the Grand Hall collapsed in a roaring display and summarily ended the broadcast. A cloud of dust arose from the great building as though a volcano had erupted on the surface.

"Destroy the planet," said Halinkoy. "I want no memory of this place to be had by anyone! And find that Warden!" Halinkoy clenched his fist and smacked it against his knee.

They gave the orders and the three Tammeder ships in orbit fired on the planet. With each shot from their canons, they wrought devastation upon the surface. The ships fired for several minutes and soon the planet broke up. The power of the Halinkoy Cult had just been put on full display.

Darbian and the children watched as the planet was

destroyed. They could hardly believe what they saw with their eyes.

Crystal Dawn was no more.

Gregorical sped away all the faster.

"Where do we go now, Darbian?" asked Hannelore

Darbian slunk over the control panel. "I know where to go. I'm not sure what we're looking for, but the last Council member gave me the coordinates. Gregorical, I'm assuming you recorded the entire conversation?"

"Of course, sir. The coordinates are programmed in and ready for your command," Gregorical said.

"Darbian, did you hear Halinkoy call my name? How could he have known who I was?" Micah's eyes darted back and forth.

"I don't know, Micah. I heard him say it, yes, but I'm not sure," Darbian responded.

"It was creepy. It was like he was surprised to see me... like he had seen me before." Micah walked off.

Darbian placed his hand on Micah's shoulder. "Thank you Micah." He looked over to Hannelore, "And thank you."

The children smiled.

"Perhaps you're more than astronauts after all," Darbian said.

"I've been trying to tell you that," Micah laughed.

Darbian's face went blank. "Micah, have you ever known anyone who disappeared?"

"What do you mean?" Micah crinkled his face.

"Anyone who mysteriously vanished? Someone never heard from again?" Darbian clarified.

"No. Why do you ask?" Micah pursed his lips.

"Nothing. It was just a thought," Darbian said. "Gregorical, will you show the children to the bunk rooms? I'm sure they need rest."

"Certainly sir," Gregorical responded.

"I'm not tired at all. I mean, I've hardly slept in two days, but I don't need any rest," Hannelore yawned.

"Trust me, after all the work you've done, you need it." Darbian pointed to the back signaling where to go.

"Might as well," responded Micah.

The children left to lie down in their bunk room.

"Sir, is there something we need to discuss on our own?" Gregorical was used to Darbian's secretive ways by now.

Darbian propped himself against the control panel. "Yes, there is, my friend. It's just a theory, and I could be wrong, but I think someone who knew Micah was among the people taken by Halinkoy. I'm not sure who it could be, but I can't think of another reason Halinkoy would recognize him."

"There's something I must tell you as well sir," said Gregorical.

Darbian stood straight, but peered towards the floor. "It's about that weapon the children were using, isn't it?"

"Yes sir," said Gregorical. "I think you will be surprised where it came from."

"I was wondering," Darbian's ears perked up.

"A time traveler boarded the ship unannounced and left it for them to use. He said nothing. He didn't identify himself. According to Micah, he looked like a Warden. The children chased him before he disappeared." Gregorical paused.

"Go on. Did you get footage of him? Surely you did," said Darbian.

"Yes I did. I said nothing to the children about it. In fact,

I directed them to hide in the heart of the ship because I didn't want them to see who it was."

"Why is that? Who was it?" Darbian put his hands on his waist and furled his brow.

Gregorical brought an image up on his screen. "It was a man in Wardein armor. I identified his face and DNA structure as matching Micah Alfero."

"So we're playing the long game," said Darbian.

"Should we tell the children, sir?" Gregorical said.

"No, I don't think so. It could impact their future in unpredictable ways, especially Micah," responded Darbian.

Gregorical replied, "Being that Micah has already visited himself, it's reasonable to assume it has already changed their future."

Darbian wiped blood from the back of his head. "Possibly, but for whatever reason Micah didn't want his younger self to know it was him. Let's go with that for now until we have a good reason to do otherwise."

CHAPTER 14

DARBIAN BROUGHT up the star maps on the main screen to study the coordinates given to him by Erevosa.

The coordinates pointed to a remote part of the universe almost devoid of stars, a good distance away from any galaxy.

Gregorical interrupted. "Shall we embark?"

Darbian's mind was consumed with thoughts about the things Halinkoy had told him. "The people that Halinkoy kidnapped...I believe they were on one of those ships. I've heard of the technology he spoke about. Some of the archives about the Tammeder speak about transmitting a person's consciousness, but it was purely experimental. The amount of power it took to transmit a person's mind was tremendous. It's not like a communications signal. There's no way those people were very far from Halinkoy himself."

"Do you think we should go back then? To attempt a rescue?" Gregorical responded.

"No, we're not ready to take on Halinkoy. What you and the children did was risky enough, not to mention irresponsible, not to mention a direct violation of my orders." Darbian pointed to the ceiling as if to scold his ship.

"You're welcome," said Gregorical.

Darbian smiled.

"To find the Astrolabe then?" Gregorical continued.

"Yes, we should proceed there immediately. There's no telling what Halinkoy has in store. We can't delay another minute." Darbian reached into his pocket and pulled out the disc that Erevosa had given him. "This should be safe to insert in to your databanks, shouldn't it?"

"Yes, I've already scanned it for corruption. You may insert it any time," Gregorical replied.

Darbian inserted the disc. "Perhaps this will tell us more about this mysterious Astrolabe."

After a few seconds, nothing had happened.

"Is it working?" Darbian asked.

"The disc is working, but there doesn't appear to be anything on it," Gregorical analyzed the disc further.

"She said we needed the disc?" Darbian was tired of questions. He wanted answers.

"Let's prepare the wormhole. We can worry about what the disc does or doesn't do later," Darbian said.

"Coming to a full stop now. Activating Chrono drive," Gregorical produced a wormhole to their most mysterious location yet, a place where neither had ever been before.

"Proceed," said Darbian.

Within an instant, the ship and its crew were transported to the remote portion of the galaxy said to harbor the Astrolabe. It was dark there as the nearest stars were millions of light years away. A few galaxies could be seen in the distance, but they appeared as dots on the horizon.

"There doesn't appear to be anything here, sir. I've

scanned a large area and I find nothing." Gregorical turned his screen on to show nothing in the area.

"What's this Secret she spoke of? I don't understand. We've done exactly as she instructed us to do." Darbian sat down and put his head in his hands.

"Sir, the disc doesn't work and there's nothing here. I hesitate to say it, but perhaps the trauma of Halinkoy's attack rendered her insane? In the first place, it makes little sense that the Council would keep any secrets from the Wardein," Gregorical said.

Darbian paused and stared at the screen for what seemed like several minutes.

Gregorical abandoned the plan rather quickly. "Sir, where should we go next?"

"Perhaps, you're right Gregorical. Perhaps we're alone after all," Darbian got up and walked to one of the bunk rooms in the back of the ship. "I think I'll get some sleep myself. I need rest to think about our next move."

"Certainly, sir," responded Gregorical.

There was little else found on this ship other than despair.

As Darbian slept, Gregorical analyzed the recordings of the conversation with Erevosa to discover any clues. He found none.

After a couple of hours, Micah woke up and walked to the bridge. "Gregorical, where's Darbian?"

"He's resting. He may be a while," Gregorical said.

"Where are we? Did we find the Astrolabe?" Micah rubbed his eyes.

Gregorical replied. "I'm afraid not, my child."

Micah's eyes tracked from one end of the bridge to another. "Are we sure we're looking in the right place?"

Suddenly, there was a knocking on the hull of the ship. Three taps and the sound was no more.

"What was that?" Micah asked.

"Something contacted my hull. Perhaps they were meteorites." Gregorical offered.

The knocking returned, this time in a pattern. It sounded reminiscent of "Twinkle Twinkle Little Star."

"That wasn't a meteorite," said Micah.

"No, it wasn't," Gregorical responded. "My sensors detect nothing. Whatever it is appears to be intelligent, however."

The knocking occurred again. This time it was steady, thump after thump.

Then on the screen appeared an object beyond Micah's imagination and beyond Gregorical's memory banks. It looked to be made of gold and comprised several interlocking rings that formed the outline of a sphere. The inner portion of the sphere appeared to be hollow. The galaxies could be seen through the other side. All along the rings were strange markings; some could be interpreted as familiar constellations. Others were unrecognizable.

Micah's gaze was fixed upon it.

Meanwhile, Gregorical had no explanation as his sensors still showed nothing present.

The rings rotated. They weren't all moving in the same direction, mind you. They each moved independently of one another as if they weren't even connected.

At that moment, the thumping stopped and Micah disappeared.

Gregorical sounded an alarm. Lights all over the ship flashed and a sharp buzzing sound reverberated through the halls.

"Darbian, wake up. Wake up now. Micah has been

taken," Gregorical said sternly as he was incapable of yelling.

Darbian roused himself. "What did you say?"

"Micah has been taken," Gregorical responded.

Hannelore had woken up too in all the madness. She came running down the hall to ask what the matter was.

"Stay in your room, Hannelore. I have to go to the bridge," said Darbian.

"But what's going on? And where's Micah?" Hannelore held back a yawn.

"I don't know, Hannelore. He's been taken." Darbian ran down the hall, but changed his mind.

"What?" Hannelore screamed.

"Wait a minute, my dear. Come with me instead. I'm sorry." Darbian took Hannelore partly because the thought of Micah disappearing had clearly scared the girl, and partly because he wanted her in his sight to protect her should whatever had taken Micah now come for her.

Hannelore shed a tear. "Darbian, you're going to get him back aren't you?"

"Yes, we will get him back," Darbian said without a shred of confidence, as he did not understand who or what could have taken the boy. The last thing he wanted, however, was for Hannelore to stew in fear.

"Gregorical, tell me what happened," Darbian said as he rounded the bend and entered the bridge.

"Sir, look at the screen," Gregorical responded.

Darbian slid and came to a stop in front of the main screen. "Where in heaven's name did that come from?"

"I'm not sure, sir. The sensors still show nothing. There was knocking on the hull and then this object appeared." Gregorical stated.

"Try to communicate with it. Send a message. Tell it we

mean no harm and we just want our friend back." Darbian scowled.

* * *

Micah appeared in a space he had never seen before and didn't understand.

It was dark except for one large light near the ceiling. The room itself was shaped like a dome with the walls covered in gears and sprockets. The floor appeared to be made of solid brass and here also were markings resembling constellations.

Micah couldn't help but think it was like being inside a giant clock.

The occasional streak of light zoomed around the walls. With each pass of light, the structure appeared to open itself and reveal star clusters and planets on the other side of the barrier.

"There are no stars that close. We're in the middle of nowhere," said Micah.

A disembodied voice echoed through the hall. "I've been waiting for you."

Micah whipped around. "Who was that?" Where am I?"

"You're in the Astrolabe and I am the Timekeeper," the voice responded.

"What is this place?" Micah asked as he looked all over for the source of the voice.

"I told you. This is the Astrolabe. Did you not seek me out?" the Timekeeper inquired.

Micah shifted from one foot to the other. "We came here to find a way to beat Halinkoy. Can you help us?"

"That will come in time," the Timekeeper said.

"I don't understand. Who are you? And how were you expecting me?" Micah roamed around the edge of the room.

"I've been watching you all your life, Micah," the Time-keeper responded.

Micah looked up in shock.

"But let's talk about these friends of yours. They keep sending me messages that they want you back. That seems like a wasted trip. Why don't I bring them here? That's a better idea, don't you think?" the Timekeeper said.

Suddenly, both Darbian and Hannelore appeared in the room alongside Micah.

"Micah! Are you okay?" Darbian shouted.

Hannelore was still crying, but calmed down when she saw her new surroundings.

"I'm fine. I'm just confused." Micah leapt over to Darbian.

Darbian grabbed Micah and hugged him. "Who's here? Why have you brought us here?" he exclaimed.

"Greetings, weary traveler," said the Timekeeper as he appeared out of the shadows and stood near a platform in the distance. He looked human. He was tall with gray hair and brown eyes, but didn't appear very old, however. Wearing a rather majestic robe, he strolled as it dragged the ground behind him. In his hand was a staff, a long, golden rod that was as tall as the one who held it. On top of the staff was a symbol that looked much like a sundial.

"Who are you?" Darbian said as he released Micah, walked forward, and pointed his wrist-bound weapon.

"I'm the Timekeeper and I believe you came here seeking me. Is that not correct?" the mysterious figure responded.

Darbian lowered his arm. "We came here seeking the Astrolabe."

"You've found it," said the Timekeeper.

"We've come here looking for a means to bring back the Wardein and defeat the Halinkoy Cult. I was sent here by Erevosa, the last member of the Council." Darbian relaxed, but glared at the man in the shadows.

"There's so much for you to learn, Darbian. So much to tell you." The Timekeeper walked closer.

"Did you tell him my name, Micah?" Darbian looked back at the boy.

"No, I didn't. But he knew mine too. Said he was waiting for me and that he had been watching me all my life," Micah trembled.

The Timekeeper stopped and reached out his hand. "Did you bring a disc with you? From the one who sent you?"

"Yes," said Darbian.

"Let me see it," said the Timekeeper.

Darbian reached into his pocket, pulled out the disc, and handed it to the Timekeeper.

The Timekeeper took the disc and walked toward a wall. As he approached, the gears moved, and a space opened. The now hollow portion was dark and looked to be nothing but emptiness. He inserted the disc, and it was swallowed up into the nothingness. The wall rippled as though he had just dropped the disc into a pool of water.

A voice, that of Erevosa, emanated through the hall. "My dear friend, Timekeeper, I'm sending to you the last Warden. He's all that remains of our force. Crystal Dawn has already fallen, and I am here to ask you for your personal aid. Please, secure him from being followed by members of the Halinkoy Cult, a vicious religious faction that seeks to rule all life in the universe. Soon, I'll tell the Warden of the Secret. He won't understand it, but perhaps in time he will. Please finish what has been started. As I leave you, I fear I won't survive the next few hours. Remember me fondly. Long live the Timekeeper."

"She's dead, isn't she?" The Timekeeper sounded somber for the first time since they met him.

"Yes, she died, but she died bravely," responded Darbian.

"Well, I've been asked to make sure no one follows you, and I'll do that. Would you like us to move so that this Halinkoy Cult doesn't arrive as well?" The Timekeeper faced Darbian.

"What? They're following us?" Darbian's eyes bugged out.

"I imagine they've been following you since you left Crystal Dawn. It's not a problem though. I'll bring your ship aboard and we'll be off." The Timekeeper was nonchalant as though avoiding the Halinkoy Cult was a small thing.

"How could you tell they were following us? Our sensors detected nothing," Darbian said.

"They've been following you from a great distance, far beyond the range of your sensors. I imagine then that their sensors are much stronger than yours if they've been able to track you all this way. No matter though; we'll leave." The Timekeeper walked toward his platform. "You might want to move."

The wall once again swirled around. The gears shifted in varying directions as Gregorical himself now appeared and moved through the water-like substance.

Safely inside the hall of the Astrolabe, Gregorical spoke. "Sir, are you alright? I've been searching frantically for you."

"We're fine, Gregorical. Are you okay?" Darbian replied.

"Quite well, sir. Never better," responded Gregorical.

Darbian looked back to the Timekeeper. "Who are you? No, really. Who are you?"

The Timekeeper looked at Darbian with a glaze in his eyes. "I'm the ghost of a race long dead. A remnant, an artifact, but a friend."

"What race?" Darbian peered though the dim light.

"Well, that's the Secret. I came from the First World," the Timekeeper responded.

"The First World?" Darbian exclaimed. "That's a legend, nothing more."

The Timekeeper smiled. "Oh no, it's very real, and you'll see it yourself one day. Of that I'm now sure."

Micah stared up at Darbian. "What's he talking about?"

"He's talking about an old legend, one of the oldest in the universe," Darbian responded.

"Yeah, go on," said Micah.

"The legend says all people everywhere came from one place...the First World. It says the people of this planet seeded the universe with life. Soon after, they fell into oblivion." Darbian rubbed his chin and looked back to the Timekeeper.

"Oh, there's more to the legend than that," said the Timekeeper.

"Is there?" Micah tugged at Darbian's arm.

Darbian huffed. "The legend also states that a child of this people was lost, but that he'll return one day and put everything right in the universe."

"So it's like a prophecy?" said Micah.

Darbian ignored Micah and approached the Timekeeper. "You seem to know certain things. Other things you don't. Why is that?"

"My purview is limited by what the Creator allows me to see," the Timekeeper responded.

"The Creator? There's no such thing," Darbian stated with confidence.

"Are you sure about that?" The Timekeeper turned back and walked to the center of the room.

"My father believed in God. I'm not sure whether I do or not," said Micah.

"That's all well and good, but..." Darbian paused.

"But what?" Micah cocked his head to the side.

"Nothing, my boy. Nothing," Darbian said.

"Perhaps you lost your belief in God when you were abandoned as a child? Wouldn't you say so, Darbian?" The Timekeeper stopped and inserted his staff into a small notch in the floor.

"What did you say?" Darbian rushed forward and grabbed the Timekeeper by the shoulder.

"I don't blame you. I probably would have doubted as well if I had lived the life you've lived. You've been abandoned, raised on a foreign world, and faced the loss of everything you hold most dear." The Timekeeper turned around.

Darbian froze. "How did you know all that?"

"Perhaps I've been watching you as well. No worries. Things are looking up!" The Timekeeper twisted his staff.

Where he stood, out of the floor came a podium. It featured an hourglass on top, ticking mechanisms all over the exterior, and a few buttons that resembled constellations.

The Timekeeper punched a few of the buttons and turned back around. "There, they'll never find us here."

Darbian looked around for signs of a ship having

budged, sounds of power, or the tug of gravity. "We've moved?"

"Yes, look for yourself," said the Timekeeper.

One of the walls moved once again, this time revealing an array of stars on the other side of the pool.

Gregorical piped in. "Yes, sir, it appears we've moved and quite far."

The Timekeeper laughed. "Yes, you could say that. We traveled 15 billion light years."

"Not possible," said Darbian.

"More than possible. Now to the mission." The Timekeeper turned and walked back to the platform.

"What mission? Stop speaking in riddles! Why are we here?" Darbian screamed louder with every question.

"Now that's a good question, my dear Darbian. One that will be answered in time. That I promise you." The Timekeeper nodded once.

"I don't want answers in time. I want to know everything right now." Spittle came out of Darbian's mouth as he spoke.

"Know this, Darbian. You have a role to play the likes of which you're not yet ready to understand. So do you, Micah! And you, Hannelore. Even you, friendly spaceship." The Timekeeper put his hands together as if to pray. "But first, come the tests."

"Tests?" Darbian had calmed down.

"You seek the means to bring back the Wardein, to defeat the Halinkoy Cult, to protect innocent life, and to find your purpose. That last one you didn't even know you were looking for. It will be given to you, all of it. But first..." The Timekeeper paused.

"Why didn't you make yourself visible when we first

arrived? We couldn't even detect you on our sensors." Darbian placed his hands on top of his head.

"Because I was waiting for Micah to wake up," the Timekeeper said.

Darbian looked at the boy. "Micah is here by accident." He faced the Timekeeper again. "He's from a planet that's yet to travel the stars. That he's with me at all is a fluke."

"Really now?" responded the Timekeeper. "Is he here by accident? Darbian, I don't believe in accidents."

CHAPTER 15

ABOARD HALINKOY'S FLAGSHIP, the self-appointed Supreme One had been rebuilding his armored suit while his soldiers sought Darbian.

A Tammeder soldier walked into Halinkoy's chamber to update him on their progress. "Supreme One, the Warden's ship has disappeared from our sensors. I'm sorry, sir, but we've lost him."

Halinkoy picked his head up. "You lost him?" He threw a piece of his armor down in a fit. "We monitored the communications between the Warden and the last Council member. What sort of incompetence does it take to lose track of that ship?"

"I'm sorry, sir. I'll sacrifice my life, Supreme One, if it pleases you. Your anger must be satisfied." The Tammeder soldier kneeled down before Halinkoy.

Halinkoy looked at him and paused for a moment. "That won't be necessary."

"Yes, my Supreme One. Thank you for sparing my life," the Tammeder soldier said.

"What would please me is the demise of the last

Warden." Halinkoy kept tinkering with his armor. "But I have a plan on how to achieve that. No more Tammeder warships, no more fighting fair. Contact Aculpus Atronis. I wish to speak to him."

"Yes, my Supreme One," the Tammeder soldier rose and exited the room. He relayed the command to the communications operators.

They went about contacting the great traitor of the Wardein.

One of the soldiers broadcasted to Aculpus' ship. "Aculpus Atronis, the Supreme One wishes to speak to you. You will answer."

The broadcast found Aculpus finishing up the destruction of Wardein Base 7713, a remote outpost. As he fired upon the base for the final time, he opened communication with the Tammeder flagship. "This is Aculpus Atronis, sworn servant to the Halinkoy Cult. I'm responding and ready to take commands from my Supreme One."

"I'll connect you with the Supreme One now," said the communicator.

Thus, Aculpus and Halinkoy were connected. Halinkoy could view Aculpus on screen, but Aculpus could not perceive two-dimensional images.

"Aculpus, my wise servant, have you finished destroying the Wardein bases?" Halinkoy asked as he put his new armor down for the first time since his old suit was stripped from him.

"Not quite, my Supreme One. I've used the Wardein databases to find all the outposts, but I haven't quite had time to finish the job," Aculpus said.

"In time, I'm sure, but I have a more important mission for you. Are you aware that the last Warden, Darbian, has escaped?" Halinkoy tapped his fingers on his knees.

Both sets of ears perked up for Aculpus. "No, my Supreme One. I wasn't told of this. I assumed he had been killed at Crystal Dawn."

Halinkoy raised his nose to the air. "I'm afraid not. He has escaped and is in search of something called the Astrolabe. Have you heard of this thing?"

"No, my Supreme One. I've never heard of it. Is it a weapon?" Aculpus clenched his teeth.

"Time will tell what it is, but it doesn't matter now. At this time, we must plot his demise, and I've already conjured a plan to do so. You'll go to Earth, the planet of my birth and the bane of my existence. Darbian cares for this place. He fears for its survival, and that makes him vulnerable." Halinkoy leaned forward. "We'll use this against him."

Aculpus put his hands together as if to clap. "Excellent, my Supreme One, what shall I do?"

"You'll proceed to the planet and broadcast a warning to Darbian that if he doesn't meet you in battle on the surface of Earth, then his beloved planet will be destroyed. My Tammeder army will arrive in orbit soon. I'm eager for a confrontation." Halinkoy smiled.

"My Supreme One, I'm honored that you would give me the opportunity to kill the last Warden. I thought, though, that you wanted to do this personally?" Aculpus bowed his head as a sign of respect.

"I won't be engaging Darbian and his young allies face-to-face. It is my will you should do this instead. It's not that I'm incapable, but I must perfect certain technologies before I go into battle again. My mind must be sharp," Halinkoy said.

Aculpus bent forward, "Are you having any troubles, my Supreme One?"

"No, you sniveling insect! I'm in perfect health. I have

discovered a weakness in the Tammeder technology, however. Not one of my creation, of course, but if my mind is connected to an individual, then I also gain their memories. If one of these memories is triggered, then my ability to concentrate is limited. The boy...the boy with the Warden, I recognized him. His father is one of the humans I captured and placed in stasis. His mind is invaluable, however, or I would remove him." Halinkoy peered at the floor and grimaced. "Darbian must never know this."

"Of course not, my Supreme One. They could exploit such a weakness," Aculpus responded.

Halinkoy stood up and screamed, "I don't have any weaknesses! The Tammeder's wisdom was limited. It is a flaw of their mind, not mine. Do you understand?"

"Yes, my Supreme One. I apologize," Aculpus replied.

"Darbian will have the children of Earth with him. Don't let your compassionate sensibilities get the best of you. Kill them as quickly as you can. They're unusually sharp and may pose a threat as I've seen in person." Halinkoy winced.

"Compassion for the useless is no longer one of my qualities," Aculpus responded.

"Good," Halinkoy said.

"Do you intend to spare the planet if he meets me in battle?" Aculpus said.

Halinkoy slammed his fist on his chair. "No! I have longed for the day when Earth would be reduced to ashes. As soon as the Warden's defeat is made sure, we'll extermi-nate the human plague from this universe. You're up to the task, aren't you, Aculpus?"

"Absolutely, my Supreme One!" Aculpus spun around in his chair and plotted a course. "I'm far more experienced in battle than young Darbian and far more committed to a just cause at that."

"Then go now. Once you've contacted the Warden, inform me. My fleet will be ready to enter the solar system as soon as we know the Warden's ship is there," Halinkoy rested in his chair once again.

"Yes my Supreme One. Long live Halinkoy!" Aculpus turned off the communication and proceeded to Earth.

* * *

Far away at the Astrolabe, the Timekeeper and Darbian continued their conversation.

"Timekeeper, the question at hand is can you help us bring back the Wardein? For now, that's all we have time to focus on." Darbian massaged his temples.

"As I said, there are tests that must be passed. A journey that must be taken." The Timekeeper continued to speak in riddles.

"What tests? We don't have time for tests," Darbian asserted. "The fate of the universe is hanging in the balance. Don't you understand that? Without the Wardein, our cause is lost. Halinkoy and the Tammeder will wreak havoc unless they're defeated soon. Whole planets will be destroyed. And you insist on playing games!"

"Ah yes, I remember the Tammeder. Nasty bunch of fighters they were," the Timekeeper reminisced.

"How could you remember the Tammeder? They've been gone for millions of years," Hannelore said as she stopped being a wallflower in this bizarre conversation.

"I'm old, my dear. I've seen peoples come and go for millions upon millions of years," the Timekeeper responded.

"You're ancient then, ageless I suppose. Almost as if the Astrolabe exists outside of time and space," Darbian theorized. "Do you think that gives you the right not to care about the people who could die?"

The Timekeeper lifted his chin. "When did I say such a thing? All people matter, all of them. The ones who are, the ones who've gone, and even the ones who've yet to come. They all matter. I know this better than even you, Darbian, and that will be plain to you soon."

Darbian smacked his fist against his palm. "Then stop playing games, old man!"

"These are no games. The tests are necessary. You must be found worthy if you are to understand the secrets of the universe. Knowledge is a terrible thing in the wrong hands, Darbian. Surely, you understand that." The Timekeeper turned and walked towards a wall.

Darbian relaxed as he had to admit the Timekeeper had a point.

"There are three tests...compassion, courage, and wisdom. These three things, Darbian, you must show them in abundance. So must Micah. So must Hannelore. You will all be tested." The Timekeeper set his staff up against the wall. "The tests will begin now. As soon as I remember where to send you that is." He winced.

Darbian threw his hands up.

"What good does it do to test us?" Hannelore said.

The Timekeeper pulled a book from the wall where there did not appear to be a bookshelf in front of him. He opened it and read to himself.

Micah shrugged. "Don't we need the Wardein? What good are we against an army?"

The Timekeeper looked back over his shoulder. "Children, do you see where the light comes from in this room?"

Darbian and the children looked up to the ceiling.

"Yeah, looks like there's one big light fixture up there," Micah said.

The Timekeeper smiled. "That's right my child. One light...and from even the darkest corners of space, it shines."

Hannelore reached out her hand towards the light. "It's not very bright though."

The Timekeeper looked down at his old dusty book. "Yes, but even a dim light is enough to read by."

"I don't get it," said Micah.

"Just a little light my child, that's all you need to do anything that's truly important," responded the Timekeeper. He then thrust his finger onto the page he was reading and popped the book as though he was crushing a spider. "Ha! I remember now where I need to send you. How delightful!"

Gregorical spoke up. "Sir, there's a message being broadcast for you. It's from Aculpus Atronis."

"Yes, I see the message now," said the Timekeeper. "You're about to be tested in a very different way I see."

Darbian leered at the Timekeeper. "Gregorical, I'll come inside and view the message there."

"Of course, sir." Gregorical then teleported Darbian and the children inside the ship.

They walked to the main screen, and the message played.

Aculpus Atronis spoke. "Darbian, my old friend. You're the last Warden, the last of a dead order. You've already been defeated, but I will give you an opportunity to regain some of your honor. At Crystal Dawn, you needed children to rescue you from certain death. I offer you the chance to face me, your former mentor, in battle. In fact, I can guarantee you'll show up because if you do not, then Halinkoy will destroy Earth, the world you care for. Meet me on the surface of that planet within the next day or your little friends will be rendered homeless."

The message repeated as it was on a loop.

Darbian stared at the screen and watched the message repeatedly even though he full well understood it the first time.

Micah glanced at the screen and then back at Darbian. "What are you going to do?"

"Children, I have to go back to Earth," Darbian said. "Halinkoy is moving the timeline. He wants to destroy the Earth now. I'm going to leave you here with the Timekeeper, however. I have to face Aculpus, but I'm not sure if I can save Earth from Halinkoy's wrath. At least you'll be safe here."

"No, Darbian, don't go alone," Hannelore cried.

"We can help you beat Aculpus," said Micah. "Vinitor tried this trick, but we figured out a way to beat him."

"No!" Darbian shed tears. "You can't help me anymore. You don't understand! I appreciate everything you've done for us, I do, but it has to end somewhere. I can't keep you safe any longer. You're so brave, but you're still children, and I've risked your lives enough. Our journey together is over. From here on out, I'm alone."

The Timekeeper appeared inside the ship. "No Darbian, you're not alone."

"What do you have to offer, old man, except more riddles?" Darbian rolled his eyes.

"Halinkoy won't stop until he destroys the Earth. This is a trap to make sure you're there when he does," the Timekeeper said.

"Yes, I know that," Darbian responded.

"Darbian, I know you don't trust me. One day you'll see

why we crossed paths. And one day you will understand why you need these children to go with you right now in this very moment." The Timekeeper tapped his staff on the floor of the ship.

Immediately, all four of them were outside the ship again and inside the hall of the Astrolabe.

"Can't the children stay with you? They'll be in danger if they go with me to Earth," Darbian responded.

"They could stay with me, yes, but you need them. Please believe me," said the Timekeeper.

Darbian glanced at the floor and then fixed his eyes on the Timekeeper. "What if I believed you? What are we supposed to do when we face Aculpus?"

"I will help you with that." The Timekeeper smiled.

"What do you intend to do?" Darbian listened.

"What you need is the Convergence," said the Timekeeper.

"The Convergence?" Micah exclaimed. "But we lost it."

"No, you lost the one from the present. I will show you how to obtain the one from the past," the Timekeeper replied.

"How are you going to do that?" asked Darbian.

"It's in my name. I'm the Time...keeper. I keep time. Haven't you been paying attention?" The Timekeeper smirked. "I'm going to send you to Armankour. At least, the version of Armankour that existed over three hundred years ago."

"Armankour is hidden. How can anyone find it?" Darbian asked.

"The Astrolabe can find anything. That's its purpose, to be a guide among the stars," the Timekeeper said.

"Tell us what to do," said Darbian.

"The Armankouri people, do you know how they hid their planet?" The Timekeeper walked back to his podium.

"Taurean said they used the Convergence to move their planet to safety. He never told me how they hid it. That would have been giving the secret away I suppose," Darbian responded.

"Oh, that's the trick." The Timekeeper punched buttons on his podium. "They moved the planet with the Convergence, yes, but they never actually hid it. They put it someplace where no one would ever look. You must repeat their plan."

The rings around the Astrolabe moved in unison. The floor itself broke into circular sections and wobbled around. Clockwork pieces on the walls turned ever so slightly and yet the gears made a great deal of clanking and squeaking as the whole room spun.

"What's happening?" Hannelore asked as her gaze shifted from one part of the room to the other.

"The Astrolabe isn't moving this time; you are," said the Timekeeper.

"Wait, wait a minute! Are you suggesting we move the planet Earth? Move it where?" Darbian screeched.

"You'll know when the time comes, Darbian." The Timekeeper spoke louder. "But, for now, I must leave you to your work. Help, yes, I can do that, but I cannot interfere in the matters of the universe," he said as he prepared to punch the final button.

"That makes no sense, Timekeeper!" Darbian was beside himself.

"You have time travel capabilities on your ship, no?" The Timekeeper pointed to Gregorical.

"Yes, of course," Darbian responded.

The Timekeeper turned around. "Alright then, once

you've taken the Convergence, then you'll have the ability to return to this time and save the Earth! You must be vigilant and brave, for soon you will be tried as never before."

"What do you mean, take the Convergence? Aren't they going to help us?" Darbian complained.

"Well, the Armankouri aren't always very generous with their revolutionary technology. I'm sure you understand. Anyway, you'll probably have to steal it," the Timekeeper said.

"Why can't you help us, you crazy old fool?" Darbian was on the verge of hitting the Timekeeper in frustration.

"I can't interfere. Godspeed weary traveler!" The Timekeeper punched the final button.

Darbian and the children disappeared along with Gregorical.

CHAPTER 16

DARBIAN AND THE children reappeared on Gregorical's bridge while the ship itself appeared in the orbit of a large planet.

Darbian shook in his chair. "Gregorical, where are we?"

"Sir, we've materialized in Prohibited Sector 17," Gregorical said.

Darbian rolled his eyes. "Are we orbiting Armankour?"

"Yes, sir, the planet fits the last known description of Armankour," Gregorical responded.

"I can't believe it," Darbian paced around the room. "They set themselves smack in the middle of Prohibition 17. Who in the blazes thought that was a good idea?"

Micah reached out to stop Darbian. "What's Prohibition 17?"

"This is a mess! I can't believe they would be this foolish. They're supposed to be the smartest people in the universe!" Darbian didn't notice Micah's question.

Micah stepped in front of Darbian this time. "Darbian, what is Prohibition 17?"

"Child, I'm sorry." Darbian stooped down to speak

to Micah. "Many generations ago, the Council of Planets deemed that certain threats were too dangerous to be contained by the Wardein alone. Instead, they devised a plan to forbid entrance into certain sectors of space. They called these sectors Prohibitions. Inside, they imprisoned whatever the threat was...anything from diseased creatures to single beings who would never be allowed to see a free universe again. They're like prisons and everyone on the outside knows you can't enter a Prohibited Sector. They're shielded from the outside to prevent it! The only way in or out is through time travel which only the Wardein and certain races possess." He stood back up. "It appears the Armankouri have tempted fate by entering one of these zones where I'm certain they hope to live without interference."

"Ok, what's special about number 17?" Hannelore piped in.

"My dear, it's hard to describe." Darbian smacked his lips. "There is a race of giants here. Oddly enough, they're peace loving. Unfortunately, they're far too large to come into contact with any other race of people. They're so immense that the sound of their voice crushes the eardrums of whoever they speak to. You don't want to know what happens to people they try to greet."

"Sir, it's best if we focus on contacting Armankour," Gregorical interjected.

"You're right." Darbian walked to the main control panel and initiated a communication. "This is Darbian...the last remaining Warden, seeking to speak to the President of the Armankouri people."

After a moment of radio silence, a voice returned. "This is the Office of the President of Armankour. How is it possible we're speaking to the last of the Wardein? We spoke to several Wardein only yesterday."

"Sir, remember, we have traveled over three hundred years into the past. The Wardein have not yet been defeated with the Time Bomb," Gregorical said.

"Yes, I forgot," Darbian said. "People of Armankour, let me restate that. I'm a Warden from the future, and I'm in desperate need of your help."

There was silence once again for a few moments, but the voice returned. "Darbian, we have no record of you occupying the office of Warden."

"Yes, as I said, I'm from three hundred years in the future. In my time, the Wardein have been defeated and I need your help to stop the culprit. The entire universe is in peril and I seek to bring back the Wardein." Darbian said.

"How did you find this planet, Darbian?" the voice returned.

Darbian inhaled, winced, and spoke. "The Timekeeper sent here us, using the Astrolabe."

Immediately, Gregorical and his passengers were teleported down to the surface.

"I'm getting a little tired of people moving me around without asking," Darbian said.

They set Gregorical and his passengers on a large platform attached to a huge tower reaching up into the sky.

The tower was a spiral that narrowed as it grew taller. Covered in glass, there were many platforms as this structure was used for visitors coming and going. It housed the government of Armankour and it was the tallest structure on the planet.

Darbian and the children disembarked the ship and walked onto the platform where they were greeted by several guards and an official of the Armankouri President.

161

"Greetings, keeper of the Secret. My name is Bau Gerean, Chief Security Officer for the President. We have awaited a representative from the Timekeeper for some time now. It's been several hundred years since he spoke to our people. Is all well?" The official spoke as though he had not heard a word of what Darbian transmitted earlier.

"No sir, nothing is well. The universe is under threat from a maniac who thinks he's a god. Your immediate help is required," Darbian responded.

Bau Gerean's face widened. "Gracious sir, what is the nature of the situation?"

"Sir, I come from a time where the Wardein have been wiped out and a cult leader named Ajax Halinkoy is holding the entire universe hostage. His ships are powerful enough to destroy planets and there's no one left to stop him," Darbian waved his arms in either direction.

"We must speak with the President and the Ruling Council," said Bau Gerean.

"There's one more thing, sir. The Tammeder have returned. Halinkoy's cult is primarily made up of Tammeder soldiers who've come back from the abyss of history. They didn't disappear, sir. They were in hibernation on Halinkoy's home planet Earth. He discovered them and has used their technology to wreak havoc. What's more is that he claims to have quadrillions of Tammeder soldiers at his disposal. In fact, sir..." Darbian paused. "Crystal Dawn has been destroyed. The Council of Planets has been eliminated along with it."

Bau Gerean stopped and stared at Darbian. "Surely, none of these things are true. These things are impossible."

"I'm afraid not, sir," Darbian responded.

Bau Gerean spoke again. "Let us go then and discover whether this is true."

The group walked into the structure and went up an elevator several stories into the Ruling Council's chambers where an emergency meeting was called to listen to this representative of the Timekeeper.

When Darbian and the children entered the room, everyone rose to their feet. The entire eleven-member Ruling Council stood to attention while the President left his desk to walk down to the floor and offer greetings.

"Darbian, representative of the Timekeeper, welcome to Armankour. We are honored by your presence and have granted you an audience here in the Rychelkour, our capital. Please, speak your mission and enlighten us," said the President.

Darbian bowed to the President. "Mr. President, I am honored to be in your presence and to be allowed to enter this iconic tower, but we come with grave news. An ancient enemy of the Armankouri has returned, Ajax Halinkoy..."

One member of the Ruling Council spoke up. "Who has spoken to you of Ajax Halinkoy?"

Darbian stepped forward. "Dignitaries, I beg your pardon and your patience. I and my companions are from the future. Three hundred years into the future to be exact. It was there we met one of your people, named Taurean, who first spoke to us of Ajax Halinkoy. Since then, we've met him face to face."

"You faced Ajax Halinkoy in person and lived to tell the story?" Another one of the Ruling Council members, Ug Jurean, said. "I don't believe it. This is nonsense."

"No need to be rude, good sir," said the President in response.

"Taurean? That's my son's name," said Bau Gerean as he laughed.

Darbian and the children peered at Bau Gerean with

surprise that their old friend was likely the child of the Chief Security Officer who had greeted them.

"Wait just a moment," another member of the Council said as he removed his glasses. "You're serious. You're actually serious."

"Yes," responded Darbian.

"What sort of Warden carries children with him?" said Ug Jurean.

Yet another member of the Ruling Council, Ti Faurean, left his seat and came down to the floor. He looked into Micah's eyes. "These are Earth children, are they not?"

"How do we know these Earth children are not accomplices of Ajax Halinkoy?" said Ug Jurean.

"You're entirely too cynical, Ug," responded the President. "The Earth people are known not to be hostile. They're not advanced enough to be so. Ajax Halinkoy is an anomaly."

"Yes, but the only one who's advanced enough has become our greatest enemy. That should tell us something," replied Ug Jurean.

"Gentlemen, Halinkoy seeks to destroy the Earth. That's the reason I've come to you at this time and place. The Timekeeper sent me to retrieve the Convergence so we may repeat the process that hid your planet and save Earth's people." Darbian put his hands together as a sign to ask the favor.

"Now, wait just a minute. You will not be allowed to take the Convergence off this planet," said Ug Jurean. "In fact, how did you know about the Convergence in the first place?"

"Because one of your people, Taurean, took it and hid it on Earth for a short period. This happens at some point in the future; I'm not sure when," Darbian said.

"No," said the President. "It's out of the question."

"We're clearly dealing with a complex web of time travel my fellow dignitaries," said Ti Faurean. "I think it's best if we let our visitor speak. He is, after all, a representative of the Timekeeper. Let's not forget that."

"He said the Tammeder had been hibernating on the native planet of Halinkoy," said Bau Gerean. "That Halinkoy had used Tammeder technology to orchestrate a reign of chaos."

"Yes, thank you, Bau. I intended for Darbian to speak. Do you mind?" Ti Faurean shot daggers through his eyes.

"Sorry, sir," replied Bau Gerean.

"Darbian, speak now. We won't interrupt any further," said Ti Faurean.

"Darbian, what is true and what is not true about what you've said?" Ug Jurean commanded.

"I'm sorry, gentlemen. I...we're in need of your help. We aren't representatives of the Timekeeper. We only met him a short time ago, and he's as mysterious to us as he is to anyone else. The coordinates of the Astrolabe were given to us by the last surviving member of the Council of Planets, shortly before she was killed." Darbian's eyes fixed on the floor.

"What is this you say?" asked the President.

"I've been trying to tell you what happened from the beginning. Have none of you been listening? I told Bau Gerean that I'm the last of the Wardein. The rest of our force has been decimated by a Time Bomb. We've been betrayed by one of our own, Aculpus Atronis. In fact, Aculpus is the one aiding Halinkoy in threatening to destroy the planet Earth. He's a member of Halinkoy's Cult and now does his bidding. The Council of Planets has been destroyed. Crystal Dawn is gone." Darbian paused. "You're our only hope of stemming the tide that Halinkoy has created. We need the Convergence!"

"The Convergence was stolen thousands of years ago," the President spoke again. "It was sold to the highest bidder by Qa Yorean, one of the scientists who designed and built it. He has since been punished, but Ajax Halinkoy was the one who obtained it and the damage he did was irreversible. A Warden of great skill and wisdom returned it to us. Ever since that time, we have moved our planet periodically to avoid detection and hide this device from any potential foe. The Convergence cannot leave Armankour. That is final."

"The Convergence is under our protection. That cursed thing has already caused enough trouble and heartache. We would destroy it if time itself wouldn't be ripped apart in all likelihood," said another member of the Council, Hed Vurean.

Darbian felt as though he were frozen in time. He sensed nothing but silence from the surrounding people. He heard nothing but the pattern of his own heartbeat. "That's how he did it."

"That's how who did what?" asked the President.

"That's how Halinkoy defeated the Wardein. When he took the Convergence, he destroyed it. That's what caused the Time Bomb," said Darbian

"How can you be sure of such a thing?" said Ti Faurean.

"It's the only thing that makes sense," said Darbian. "If destroying the Convergence would rip apart time then that's precisely what Halinkoy has done. You said yourself that Halinkoy has caused great irreversible harm."

"Irreversible harm? Does that mean the Wardein are gone forever?" Hannelore picked up on an important detail.

"No! It can't mean that!" Darbian responded not knowing if he was telling the truth or not.

Ug Jurean responded. "That's not possible. If Halinkoy destroyed the Convergence upon buying it then how could it have been returned to us? That's obviously not what happened!"

"Not necessarily," said Bau Gerean. "There have always been rumors they created more than one Convergence device."

"Bau, would you please be quiet?" the President huffed.

Ti Faurean spoke up. "Now good sirs, let us consider what is being said here. If we're dealing with a complex series of events interconnected through time, then we can't be precisely sure of what's happened and what hasn't. More importantly, we can't interfere in these events. Perhaps the Convergence was returned to us after having been used to decimate the Wardein. Perhaps its secrets are not fully understood, even by us."

Ug Jurean jumped to his feet. "Unless, of course, these travelers plan on procuring the Convergence so they may give it back to Halinkoy and then he could use it to do whatever he wishes...perhaps even destroy the Wardein. There's no reason to trust these people."

Ti Faurean stood up. "Why would these people do any of those things? It would do nothing but raise suspicion to speak of the Convergence in such a way. How else would they have found our planet if not guided here by the Timekeeper? The fact of the matter is that this tragedy has already happened. We can't stop it by refusing to cooperate. We'll only damage our own history if we try to rewrite the future."

"Ah, yes, but the future is never written in stone," said the President.

"I understand," said Ti Faurean. "But what if it's destiny that these travelers receive the Convergence now so they may use it and return it at a time in the past?"

"That's not possible," said Hed Vurean. "The Convergence we have now is the one that was returned in the past. Where it goes from here is a future event, not a matter of history."

"I hate time travel," said Hannelore.

"Are we sure of this?" said Ti Faurean. "Is it not possible they used the Convergence to move the planet Earth in a future time? In all of our investigation we have never known the key point in the series of events that led to Qa Yorean selling the device. These events could be completely unrelated."

"But what is the proof? We must have proof or we could, in fact, be damaging the timeline further," said Ug Jurean.

"Hear! Hear!" said many of the Ruling Council.

"Warden Darbian, you said the Convergence was taken by an Armankouri scientist named Taurean at some point in the future. In fact, you said it was taken to Earth. Where's the device in your time? Why couldn't you use it then?" asked Hed Vurean

Darbian sniffed. "Well, that's a funny story."

"Is it now?" said Ug Jurean.

"The truth is...that...uh...we don't know where the Convergence is. We were trying to protect it from Vinitor, a bounty hunter working for Halinkoy, and Taurean programmed it to relocate with no direction or record of where it went." Darbian put his hands behind his back as though he were a child about to be scolded by his teacher.

"You can't be serious," said the President. "You've

already lost it once and you want to lose it again? We should kick you off this planet right now!"

"Hear! Hear!" said a few of the Council members.

"Let's not be hasty," said Ti Faurean. "Where is this scientist you speak of, this Taurean? Perhaps he has an explanation for what he did?"

"Well, he's currently stuck inside a time dilation field," said Darbian.

"I see," said Ti Faurean.

"Taurean said you move the Convergence periodically to keep secret its location..." Darbian said.

Ug Jurean interrupted. "This Taurean sounds irresponsible. In addition to his folly of allowing the Convergence to be lost, he's profoundly mistaken. We would never move the Convergence from place to place. That's the height of foolishness. We keep it on Armankour and move the planet itself from time to time."

"Actually, that's just what we tell the Council. We move it all the time at the order of the President," said a grinning Bau Gerean.

The President put his hand over his forehead.

"Excuse me?" said Ug Jurean as he nearly fainted.

Other Council members mumbled and grumbled as well.

The President composed himself and stood to his feet. "I'm sorry, good sirs, but ever since the Convergence was first stolen, there has been a secret Presidential program to keep it on the move throughout the universe. The betrayal of Qa Yorean proved we had to keep it safe from ever our own people."

"Secret program?" Hed Vurean asked as he flipped through a pile of papers laying on the desk in front of him.

"If you're looking for a memo, you won't find one," said the President.

"It can't be very secret if blabbermouth Bau Gerean knows about it!" said Ug Jurean.

"Master Vurean, legally, I didn't have to tell every member of the Council, only one was necessary," said the President.

"Who didn't inform the rest of the Council?" Ug Jurean shouted out.

The members argued with each other and accused each other of being the culprit and the accomplice to the President's deceit. Within a moment, all eyes settled on Por Winean, another member of the Council.

Por Winean was unusually short and pudgy, even for an Armankouri. He had unusually large teeth, wore large thick glasses, and was widely regarded as the dumbest member of the Council. His father, who was one of the great leaders in Armankouri history, helped him get the position.

"Por Winean, you foolish, foolish creature!" said Ug Jurean.

"What? I enjoyed being in the loop for once," said Por Winean.

"It's no matter now," said the President. "The secret is out and I might as well tell the rest of you that the Convergence isn't on Armankour. Now, that makes no difference to you, Darbian. I will not tell you the location so you can retrieve it."

"You don't understand. The Earth will be destroyed! We have no way of fighting off Halinkoy and his army. I would ask you for weapons, but I know you have none," Darbian argued.

"Is that meant to be sarcastic?" asked Ug Jurean. "Do you think we care nothing of protecting our own people?"

"That's not what I was implying," said Darbian.

"The Wardein were created to protect the innocent peoples of the universe. This isn't our responsibility. Do your job, Warden." The President walked back to his desk and sat down.

"There are no Wardein, aren't you listening?" Darbian shouted. "I'm alone against a madman and an army of Tammeder!"

The President relaxed in his chair. "Bau Gerean, please escort our guests back to their ship. We have no further business with them."

Bau Gerean and his deputies escorted Darbian and the children away.

Micah pulled away for a moment and stepped forward. "You're really not going to help us?"

"No," said the President. "I'm sure you'll find another way, though. Good luck and peace to you."

"Come along now," Bau Gerean sighed.

Darbian and the children walked out of the room and back to the platform that Gregorical was resting on.

Bau Gerean looked up at Darbian and motioned for him to bend down.

Darbian did so.

"I have a surprise for you," whispered Bau Gerean. "My office is responsible for hiding the Convergence, and I'm going to show you where it is."

"You are? Why would you do that?" whispered Darbian.

Bau Gerean continued. "Because you know my son. At least, you know him in the future and...he trusted you. My son isn't full grown now, but he's a wonderful judge of character. If he trusted you, then I know I can trust you."

Darbian grabbed the hand of Bau Gerean. "What do you want us to do?"

"I want you to run for your ship. I will follow you, but I have to distract my deputies first. If I give them an order to help, I know they won't," Bau Gerean responded. "Go now."

Darbian ran and called for the children to follow closely.

One deputy cocked his neck. "Why are they doing that?"

Meanwhile Bau Gerean took out his stun weapon and fired it at each of his deputies, knocking each of them out. "Time to run. I hope I don't regret this!"

Darbian, the children, and Bau Gerean boarded the ship.

"Take off, Gregorical; we have a new destination!" Darbian said.

Gregorical took off in quite a hurry, engaged his Galacto drive, and left the planet before any of the Armankouri realized what had happened.

CHAPTER 17

DARBIAN TURNED to his new Armankouri friend, "Where are we going?"

"To a very special place, a city that's always on the move," said Bau Gerean

"If it's always on the move then how can you tell where it is?" Micah said.

"I'll see to that young one; all we need to do is proceed to the Eukarypto galaxy," replied Bau.

"How do we get out of the Prohibited Sector though? Are we time traveling?" Darbian gestured for Bau to answer.

"Normally, we would time travel, yes, but the Armankouri have a way around the shielding," said Bau

Gregorical interrupted. "It appears there several ships following us from Armankour. Five to be precise."

"Oh, yes, that's the security force coming to capture us and bring us back to the planet," said Bau.

"The what?" Darbian griped.

"Didn't I tell you they would follow us? Perhaps I should have mentioned that," said Bau.

Darbian shook his head. "Yes, that would've been helpful."

"They know I've come with you and that I wasn't authorized to leave the planet. Sneaking away might have been better, but my guards would have informed on me anyway if I had left my post. Besides, we were supposed to escort you back to orbit and away from the planet. That's our protocol," Bau nodded and chuckled.

"Okay, just tell us how to get around the shielding," Darbian moved on.

"Well, you don't go around it. You go through it at a certain speed," Bau stated.

"Fly through it? Well, that's suicide!" Darbian flailed his arms.

"Darbian, I'm sure you're aware that the Armankouri designed the shielding. We knew what we were doing, my good man." Bau put his hand up near his mouth as though he were about to whisper. "All you have to do is achieve the speed of light. Think about it, nothing can get through that shielding except light itself. Travel at precisely the speed of light and you'll pass through the shield as though it weren't even there. It's so simple, it's brilliant."

"It is brilliant, I suppose," replied Darbian.

"And quite intuitive. How else would the starlight penetrate the shields?" Bau grinned. "A smart people indeed."

"You heard him, Gregorical. Eukarypto it is," said Darbian.

Gregorical engaged his Galacto drive and set it at light speed.

After a few moments, they reached the shielding and penetrated it without a problem. Once on the other side, they could see the other Armankouri ships had followed them through the shielding.

"Use the wormhole generator, Gregorical. Perhaps we'll lose them for a time at least," said Darbian.

"Yes, good plan. Those ships likely don't possess Chrono drives." said Bau.

Gregorical generated a wormhole meant for the heart of the Eukarypto galaxy. He flew through it and popped out in the middle of their destination.

"Where to now, my friend?" said Darbian.

"The Asteroid City flies nearest to the great asteroid belt. That's where we're going. And the great asteroid belt encircles the entire galaxy at approximately two thirds its depth, going outward!" Bau cleared his throat.

"Superb Bau. I'm sorry I doubted you," replied Darbian.

Bau patted his belly several times. "Happy to be of service, sir. Armankouri Security is the best security. You should remember that."

"I think I've heard of the Asteroid City. It's one of the richest places in the entire universe. It's bustling with commerce because they constantly travel to their customers rather than wait for people to come to them." Darbian placed his fingers on the control panel and pulled up files on the Asteroid City.

"Exactly, good sir. They fly among the asteroids and the small planets of the outer rim. It's the perfect place to hide a technology as valuable as the Convergence because everyone would expect nothing but valuable items to be in such a place. Therefore, they think, no one would risk putting such a device in the open. They would think it's better to hide it in a secret place...so no one comes looking for it," said Bau.

Gregorical flew at high speed toward the great asteroid belt, arriving in only a few minutes.

"Now, how do we find the Asteroid City? It's still a large search area," remarked Darbian.

"That's the simple part. We don't have to find them. They'll find us. All we must do is transmit a message and tell them we're in the market for jagotanium deposits. It's a rare metal in this part of the universe, and Asteroid City is one of the few places you can find it. Good plan, no?" Bau smirked.

"Yes, but what are they going to do when we can't buy any of it? We have no money!" Darbian was ever practical.

"They'll be more than happy to let us shop in the city for free. And I know precisely where the Convergence is," said Bau.

Darbian raised his eyebrow. "Does the government of Asteroid City know where the Convergence is?"

"Oh no. We never tell the people we're hiding it among that it's in their possession. That would make the situation entirely too dangerous. People in the government or others, for that matter, might be tempted to use it for their own ends," Bau replied.

Darbian glared at Bau. "So what if we get in trouble with the City?"

Bau grabbed Darbian's hand. "Don't worry about that, Darbian. The Convergence is well hidden and my contact there is a good friend. We can trust him to keep our secret."

"Excellent...I guess." said Darbian. "This might not be so hard after all."

Bau Gerean transmitted a message to the Asteroid City's merchants requesting a sale of jagotanium.

They responded, and within a few minutes, the city had arrived in the presence of Gregorical and the crew.

Asteroid City was a magnificent sight. Made from a forty-mile-long, nine-mile-wide, and fourteen-mile-high asteroid; it nevertheless moved as nimbly as any small fighter. Within the heart of it was a bustling city filled with over seven million people from different planets and galaxies. On the top of the asteroid was a tower with a disc at its center, this was the location of the bridge. At certain places, artificial structures protruded from the sides of the asteroid, each with windows to allow the residents to peer out into the stars. The edges were rounded off and used to incorporate engines in every conceivable corner of the ship. There were dozens of platforms on each side of the rock ready to receive travelers.

On one platform, Gregorical came to rest. A large bay door opened into the asteroid and Gregorical was slowly pulled inside. The bay door closed behind them.

Bau Gerean leapt up. "Follow me now, we should be quick about this."

They all departed the ship and as soon as they approached the outer door, they were met by a dozen merchants towing barrels of jagotanium behind them.

"Hello, good sirs," started Bau Gerean. "I apologize, but we have no money. We were so desperate to see your stunning city that we just couldn't resist finding a reason to get aboard."

The merchants frowned in unison.

A couple of them threw down the handle of their carts in frustration.

"Very well then," one of them said.

The children shrugged their shoulders.

Darbian gulped. "Very forward of you Bau."

Bau, Darbian, and the children walked through multiple corridors, past numerous shops, and even through the famous Diameter Square at the heart of the city.

Darbian grumbled. "Where exactly are we going, Bau?"

"We're going to the engine room. That's where that friend of mine works. He knows how to access the Convergence from his post," Bau said.

Just as Bau, Darbian, and the children entered the engine room near the rear of the ship, they saw a shocking sight.

The Armankouri security force that had followed them off the planet had somehow beaten them to the station. Dozens of them were standing inside the engine room.

"Oh dear, I didn't expect that," Bau said.

The new chief security officer spoke. "Bau Gerean, you've betrayed the trust of the President of Armankour. You're to be arrested and imprisoned immediately. Your accomplices will also be arrested."

"This is for the good of the universe; don't you see that?" Darbian implored.

"The Convergence is under the protection of the Armankouri people. It will never be allowed to leave our possession," the security officer spoke.

Each of the officers pointed their stun weapons at Bau, Darbian, and the children.

"Will you be coming along peacefully? Or do we have to stun you?" the security officer asked.

Bau hung his head.

Darbian propped himself up against the corridor and tapped the walls. "Do you even know whether the Convergence is here?"

"Of course, it's here," said the security officer.

"Well, I don't believe you. You can't arrest us for stealing the Convergence when we clearly don't have it in our possession. If it's not even here, then how would you prove we came here to get it?" Darbian said.

Bau Gerean picked up on what Darbian was angling at.

"Exactly, Armankouri law forbids arrest unless a crime has been committed."

"A crime has been committed. You left your post, Bau Gerean," the security officer said.

"That's not a crime. That's dereliction of duty; there's a difference. You may bring me back to Armankour, but Darbian and these children did nothing wrong. By law, you must let them go." Bau perched his hands on his hips and smiled.

"A crime is in process. You're all here to steal the Convergence. Why else would you be in Asteroid City? Why else would you be in the engine room where the device is kept?" The security officer continued.

Darbian interjected. "Alright then, prove to us that the Convergence is here. Show it to us!"

"I'm not going to show it to you. Everyone here knows the Convergence is in this room. Stop playing games and come along peacefully." The security officer insisted.

"The Convergence could be here, I guess, but I've never even seen it before," said Micah.

"You'll just have to show it to us if you want to arrest us," said Hannelore.

"You'll have to move it anyway since everyone knows where it is now," said Darbian smirked.

"Oh fine then. If it means you'll come along peacefully, then I'll show you the Convergence. Lieutenant, retrieve the Convergence from the utility closet," barked the chief security officer.

Hannelore craned her neck. "That's where you hid it? Anybody could find it there."

"That shows you how little you understand, young one. It was hidden under the mop bucket, and it's clear that no one mops this filthy engine room floor," said the security officer.

The Lieutenant opened the utility closet, pulled out the Convergence, and brought it back to the chief security officer.

The security officer took the Convergence and held it up. "You see here. The Convergence is indeed here. You already knew that, of course. You're here to steal it, everyone knows that." He flailed his arms about. "Now that the law has been fulfilled, we're going to arrest you. Please come peacefully or we'll be forced to stun you."

Darbian threw his hands up as though he were about to surrender. "One more request, my good sir."

"Oh, what is it now?" the security officer said.

"In order to be arrested for stealing the Convergence, I have to be holding the Convergence. Am I not correct?" Darbian looked to Bau for confirmation.

"He's right. Someone must actually hold the Convergence before they could be accused of stealing it," replied Bau.

"Fine. Come here, and hold the Convergence," said the security officer.

"Thank you," said Darbian as he walked toward the security officer and picked up the Convergence.

"I must say, you're a terrible Warden. A good one would never have involved himself in all this nonsense. At that, a good Warden would never have been so persnickety if he had been found in the wrong," the security officer complained.

Darbian held the Convergence and examined it while the officer lectured.

"Are you quite done, Warden? We've wasted entirely

too much time on this exercise as it is," said the security officer.

"I think you're right. We've wasted a lot of time we simply don't have." Darbian spoke into his communicator. "Gregorical, alert the Asteroid City authorities that this Armankouri security force has hidden a dangerous device in the engine room without their permission. We've recovered it and need safe passage to return it the proper authorities."

"Absolutely, sir," replied Gregorical.

"What?" cried the security officer. "You won't get away with that."

"Yes, we will," replied Bau.

Within a few seconds, guards working for Asteroid City showed up in the engine room. Upon noticing that the only Warden in the room had the Convergence and that it was his ship Gregorical that had informed them of the situation, they trusted Darbian's account of the events.

"Armankouri security force, you've entered our city without permission and taken advantage of our hospitality by hiding a dangerous artifact within our sovereign space. You're under arrest!" the Asteroid City chief guard stated.

"That's not at all what happened. You don't understand!" said the Armankouri security officer. "We hid it here for safekeeping. No one was in danger."

"That's an argument you'll have to make to the magistrate. Come with us immediately." The Asteroid City guards pointed their weapons at the Armankouri security force.

"You're in a terrible amount of trouble, Bau Gerean! Every move you've made has made the situation worse for you," the Armankouri security officer said.

"It's quite alright. I'll pay off my debt in due time," said Bau.

The Asteroid City guard reached out to shake Darbian's hand. "Warden, thank you for your service to Asteroid City. Do you need assistance getting back to your ship?"

Darbian extended his hand as well, and they shook.

"No, my friend. We're alright from here. We just need our ship to be given quick permission to exit the docking bay," said Darbian.

"You'll be given that immediately, Warden. Good fortune to you!" said the Asteroid City guard. "And, by the way, if you'd like 500 free units of Asteroidies to shop aboard the ship then feel free to take advantage of that at any time. I'll make a record of your service. Just drop by the Bank and offer your identification."

"Thank you, that's most generous," replied Darbian.

Darbian, Bau, and the children left the engine room and rushed back to the bay where Gregorical was docked. They boarded the ship and left Asteroid City.

Micah glimpsed the City on the screen as it passed into the night. "So how much is 500 Asteroidies?"

"I have no idea," replied Darbian.

"Maybe next time we can get a snack if we drop by," said Hannelore.

Darbian put his hand on Bau's back. "At some point you must go back to Armankour, Bau, but are you coming with us for now?"

"No, Darbian, I need you to return me to Armankour. I'll face discipline, but I want you to promise me it won't be in vain. I've risked my career and my family's place for you. Don't allow my trust to be misplaced," said Bau.

"It won't be; I assure you." Darbian nodded. "My friend, you've helped us save a planet and maybe even more than that. I'll be forever grateful to you."

"Another thing, Darbian. You've never used the

Convergence before. You must understand its secrets. Understand that wherever you plan to hide the Earth, you must ensure that Halinkoy cannot follow you," Bau said.

"Certainly, that's the plan," Darbian replied.

"No, you don't understand. When someone moves through time and space with the Convergence, a signature is left. Someone with ill intentions could use that signature to discover where the Convergence has taken you. You've noticed that Armankouri rarely leave their planet. The reason is that we fear capture by our enemies. If any of our enemies were to detain us, then they could discover the location of our planet. We have to be very careful when and where we go. But you Darbian, you need to be in space at all times. The universe is depending upon you to engage Halinkoy and defeat him. You can't afford to be on the Earth when it is moved," Bau said.

"I understand now. I must leave the Earth behind before the device is activated. Thank you for telling me this," said Darbian.

"Not only that, but keep in mind that if you were to be captured by Halinkoy, then perhaps he could coax the location out of you. These things are possible," said Bau.

Darbian bowed his head. "How do the Armankouri keep from giving away the location of their planet in the event you're captured?"

"We're never captured. The ability to morph into other creatures comes in handy. We hide ourselves when we leave Armankour. That and we have to be given permission to leave the planet. It's very rare to encounter an Armankouri these days, unless they're on official business," said Bau.

Darbian thought back to the capture of his friend Taurean. He dared not reveal that secret as it was a future event for Bau Gerean and his people. Darbian remembered that Taurean was all too willing to give up the Convergence to protect the people of Earth from destruction. Of course, the encounter with Vinitor worked out for the best, but Darbian also understood the fine line that must be walked when it came to the stakes of this game.

"You're right. I've only met a few Armankouri in my travels of the universe and the meetings were always brief," replied Darbian.

"That's not an option for you, Darbian. Again, you must travel the stars and discover a way to bring back the Wardein and defeat Halinkoy. I wish you luck, but it rests on you to be wise. No one else can be that for you," said Bau.

"Halinkoy is cunning enough to put me in a position to reveal the location of Earth. I can see that coming," said Darbian.

"Be wise, Darbian," replied Bau.

Darbian looked at the main screen and gazed at the stars passing by. "I know what I must do. I must allow the Convergence to take Earth wherever it may and I can never know where. Once the Earth has been moved, it will be lost to me forever. There's no other way."

CHAPTER 18

GREGORICAL PASSED through the Prohibition 17 shielding once more and returned to an orbit over Armankour.

"Goodbye, my friends; I wish you the best of luck on your journey. I suppose I'll never know if you are successful. The future is something I'll never see. But the Timekeeper chooses well. Be safe," said Bau.

"Goodbye, Bau Gerean. Perhaps we'll meet again," replied Darbian.

This time, Darbian didn't communicate with the Ruling Council or the President. He didn't seek permission to land, but gave Gregorical the order to make as swift a trip to the surface as possible.

Gregorical dove to the planet and landed in a park in the middle of the capital city.

Bau Gerean departed the craft with haste as he waved goodbye.

Gregorical took off again before any security ships could seize him. He sped through the atmosphere and away from Armankour.

Darbian sat down for the first time in quite a while. "Gregorical, it's time we went to Earth. Is the Chrono drive ready to time travel?"

"Yes, sir. Shall I engage it now?" Gregorical replied.

"Yes. After we've traveled back to the correct time, please generate a wormhole to get back to Earth as soon as you can. I'm about to enter the battle of my life. Might as well get it over with," Darbian said.

"You were talking with Bau about leaving the Earth behind forever. We can't leave Earth," said Micah. "It has to be protected."

"And we have to see our parents again," said Hannelore.

"We'll talk about it later, children," replied Darbian.

"We should talk about it now. Come up with another way. We can't leave the Earth," said Micah.

"No, children, you're not coming with me. I've had no chance to bring you back home safely, but soon I'll be able to do that. I'm a Warden, and that's no life for a child. It's far too dangerous and I've taken too many risks as it is. You're getting the chance to go back home. Be happy," Darbian said.

"We're not children," said Hannelore.

"What?" quipped Darbian.

"We're in middle school. We're teenagers, not children," replied Hannelore.

Darbian looked down at Hannelore. "My dear—"

She interrupted. "I'm not your dear. You keep calling us children even though we've helped you an awful lot the last few days. You wouldn't have made it this far without us."

"I suppose you're right, my...my girl," Darbian corrected himself.

"And the Timekeeper said you needed us," Micah said.

"The Timekeeper said I needed to bring you to Earth to

help me hide it." Darbian turned his face away from the children. "He never said you shouldn't go back home."

"What he said is that we had to be tested," replied Hannelore. "How do you think we're supposed to do that back home?"

"I don't know, Hannelore, but don't you understand what's happening?" Darbian raised his voice. "I will probably die soon, one way or the other. I have to save the Earth here and now because it's the only thing I can do...one small victory, but it's a victory, nonetheless. Protect it and protect you; that's what I've got to do because that's what I've sworn to do. Someone else will have to take up the fight when I'm gone though. One man against an army, it's not going to work."

"Show me how to be a Warden," said Micah.

"What?" replied Darbian.

Micah stood up straight as if at attention. "I want to be a Warden. You don't have to be alone."

"Me too," said Hannelore. "The more the merrier."

Darbian smacked the arms of his chair. "And who will train you? The Wardein are gone...no more drill sergeants...no more junior training camps. Morolith itself might be gone by now. Who knows how far Halinkoy has come."

"You could train us," said Micah.

"Haven't you heard? The last Warden is the weakest Warden. For me to train you wouldn't do any good." Darbian's eyes gravitated to the floor.

"Where do you think Micah learns to be a Warden if not from you?" The Timekeeper appeared, seated on the other side of the central workstation.

Darbian looked up. "Where did you come from?" Moving his head from side to side, he noticed that everything and everyone around him had frozen except for the Timekeeper.

Micah and Hannelore were standing like statues. Not a muscle moved.

The ship's sounds of power were gone.

There were normally a few flashing buttons spread about the bridge, but all fell still.

Darbian jerked up out of his chair. "How did you do that?"

The Timekeeper waved his finger back and forth. "Time...keeper, still not paying attention, eh?"

"What do you want with us now?" Darbian said.

"I don't want anything. I'm here to help you," the Time-keeper replied.

Darbian put his hands on his hips. "We have the Convergence. We're going to Earth and to move it like you said."

"Good, but that's not why I'm here," replied the Timekeeper.

"What else do we need to do?" Darbian said.

"Not quit," the Timekeeper said.

"I didn't come this far to quit." Darbian turned around and sat back down.

"Really? Then why are you planning on laying down and dying?" The Timekeeper scratched his chin.

"I'm not quitting. When we move the Earth, I will engage Halinkoy and probably die in the process. I'm a real-ist," said Darbian.

The Timekeeper pointed at the children with his staff. "What was it I asked you earlier? Where do you think Micah learns how to be a Warden if not from you?"

"I have no idea. He's too young to fight. They both are. I can't teach them or wait for them to grow. There's no time!

And you're missing the obvious, there's only one of me." Darbian pointed to his own chest.

The Timekeeper set his staff down and leaned on it. "Darbian, what's the definition of a Warden? What does the word mean?"

Darbian took a deep breath. "The Wardein were tasked with protecting the known universe from the threat of..."

"No, no. I'm not talking about all that. I'm talking about the word." The Timekeeper pounded his staff on the floor. "What about the word itself?"

"I've never thought of it any other way," replied Darbian.

"A person who has been entrusted with the oversight of something important. That's what it means," said the Timekeeper.

"Yes, I suppose so," replied Darbian.

The Timekeeper pointed to the children again. "Don't you think they're important?"

"Of course, that's why I'm taking them back home so they won't be in any more danger," Darbian said.

The Timekeeper shook his head. "You must face Halinkoy today. That is true, but the danger doesn't end there...for them or for anyone else. Stop feeling sorry for yourself and use your head, Darbian."

Darbian gritted his teeth.

"I've been doing some investigating. This doesn't begin or end with Halinkoy. He can wait. There's no reason to go charging after him," said the Timekeeper.

"What are you talking about?" Darbian said.

"An ancient enemy is at work, a timeless evil. I can't say much more about it now, but the point is that you are needed and those children are needed," said the Timekeeper.

"I'm weak, Timekeeper. It's dumb luck I'm even still alive," replied Darbian.

"Oh, did you listen to all that nonsense from Halinkoy?" The Timekeeper pounded the floor again. "You're chosen, but not by him and not by Aculpus and not by any other arrogant jerk that's plaguing the universe."

"I can't fight evil by myself," said Darbian.

"You're not supposed to," replied the Timekeeper. "Yes, it's true. You're weak, but you're a person. You're supposed to be weak. You are strong are in so many other ways. And that's what you have to teach them...how to overcome the weakness."

"You want me to take them with me?" Darbian said.

"Yes, Darbian. They need you and just as important, you need them. I already told you that, but you weren't listening. I can't blame you though. Perhaps your brain is a little too scrambled."

"What's that?" said Darbian.

"Two sets of memories? You should get that looked at," said the Timekeeper.

"Well, we can't just go back to Earth and do nothing," said Hannelore.

Darbian realized in that instant that the Timekeeper had disappeared and that everyone else was unfrozen. "Did I dream that?"

"Sir, are you ok?" Gregorical said.

"I'm fine, Gregorical." Darbian walked around the bridge for a moment.

"We have to go with you, Darbian. You need our help," said Micah.

Darbian massaged his eyes. "Gregorical, it's time to go."

"You're ignoring us," said Hannelore.

"I'm not ignoring you. I'm thinking," replied Darbian.

Gregorical engaged the Chrono drive and time traveled three hundred years into the future.

"Armankour isn't there anymore. They've moved it since we left. It looks like they get the Convergence back after all," said Darbian.

"Well, that means we don't leave the Earth behind. Doesn't it?" Micah said.

"What do you mean?" replied Darbian.

"If the Convergence was used to move Earth, then we must have gone with it. Otherwise, how would they get the Convergence back?" Micah shrugged.

"Maybe they built another one," Hannelore said.

"Yes, they probably just built another one," replied Darbian. "Bau said there were more of them out there. Come now, there's work to do. Gregorical, take us out of the Prohibited Sector."

Gregorical engaged light speed and left Prohibition 17.

"Earth is next Gregorical, but before you go, I want to give some final instructions to the children...teenagers," said Darbian.

Hannelore turned her back.

"You were right. I never would have made it this far without your help, and I want to thank you for that. But I need you to be brave now...maybe braver than you've ever been." Darbian paused. "I'm about to fight my mentor. He's probably already on Earth waiting for me. In a few moments, I will drop you back in your city where I found you and I need your help to prepare the Convergence. Gregorical will help you with that."

Micah clasped his hands together. "And?"

Darbian threw his hands up. "And after that, I'm not sure. I will not quit, but I don't know what's going to happen next. It's possible that Aculpus will kill me and I'll never see you again."

Micah cried.

"Come now, my boy; teenagers don't cry," Darbian said.

"Yes, they do," said Hannelore as she turned around with tears in her eyes. "My dad told me so."

Darbian turned away. "Gregorical, are you ready to go back to Earth?"

"Yes, sir. I am ready for whatever comes," replied Gregorical.

Darbian straightened his back. "Let's go then, my friend, to whatever fate awaits us."

Gregorical engaged the Chrono drive once again and generated a wormhole back to Earth.

Within a couple of minutes, they were in Earth's orbit.

In the distance, Aculpus Atronis' ship was also orbiting the planet.

"We're receiving a message, Darbian," said Gregorical.

"I imagine it's from Aculpus. Gregorical, put it through," replied Darbian.

Aculpus appeared on Gregorical's main screen.

"Darbian, I was beginning to think you wouldn't come, that perhaps you had become a coward," Aculpus said.

"The only coward here is you, Aculpus. You betrayed your brotherhood and your entire life's work. And you did it for what? To serve a madman?" Darbian said.

"I betrayed no one. I realized how hollow and weak the Wardein were. They had no ability to make the universe what it should be. I found a better way. I found the Halinkoy Cult, and I'm all the happier for it," Aculpus retorted.

"Making the universe what it should be? What exactly should the universe be, Aculpus? And how does helping a madman destroy innocent lives achieve it?" Darbian's yelled.

"Ha! The Wardein were useless. After millions of years of their existence, the universe was still a chaotic place. Hypocrites! They said they stood for decency and justice, but they accomplished nothing. There was no great order, no peace, and no freedom from war. Soon, those things will be a reality because Halinkoy will simply destroy whoever doesn't submit," Aculpus said.

Darbian shook his head. "Your mind has been twisted, Aculpus. How could you have done the things you've done? You betrayed us all. How could you have betrayed me, your friend?"

"You try to appeal with friendship? You're a pathetic, sentimental creature. I will enjoy destroying you. Yes, I think I will. I'll bask in the glory of killing the last Warden!" Aculpus said.

"So be it, old friend. If I must destroy you to protect the innocent people of Earth, then I must do my duty," replied Darbian.

"Good. I challenge you to a battle in the tradition of the Rites of Morolith," said Aculpus.

"You have no right to challenge me to such a fight. You've forsaken your office of Warden. The Rites of Morolith are for those who have honor," responded Darbian.

"Ah, but you have an obligation to accept, you miserable peon. You are honor-bound to fight me in such a way," said Aculpus.

"Meet me in Garden City," said Darbian. "Follow me down if you're not sure where it is."

"I can't wait. To the death!" Aculpus cut off the communication.

"What are the Rites of Morolith?" asked Micah.

"It's an ancient tradition among the Wardein. You meet one of your fellow Wardein in battle, hand to hand combat...no weapons. Whoever wins the battle has the right to demand anything he wishes of the loser," replied Darbian.

"I don't understand. He said he wanted to kill you," said Hannelore. "What would he want you to give him?"

"It's a trick of some sort, my girl. I don't know what he wants, but he desires some final dishonor from me. Hopefully, it won't matter," replied Darbian.

"Sir, would you like me to land in Garden City as you said?" Gregorical said.

"Yes, Gregorical. The first thing I will do is drop the children off with their families. Then I'll meet Aculpus in battle," Darbian responded.

Gregorical flew down to Earth's surface and hovered just above the streets of Garden City.

"Wow, I almost didn't expect to see this place again," said Micah.

"I don't remember it being this beautiful," remarked Hannelore.

"Children...teenagers, tell me where you live and we'll go there immediately," said Darbian.

"Over there," Micah pointed. "We live in the historic district on the east side of town."

"Be quick, Gregorical. Aculpus will follow us soon," said Darbian.

Gregorical darted to the area Micah pointed toward. He landed just down the street from their houses.

The neighbors all came out shouting and screaming.

"Another ship has landed!" one of them cried.

"I think I've seen that one before," said another.

The children ran off the ship and to their respective houses.

Micah's mother, Elizabeth, and Hannelore's father, Brendan, ran out of their houses as they saw the children approaching.

"Micah! Where have you been?" Elizabeth cried profusely. "I thought I'd lost you forever."

"Mom!" cried Micah.

She hugged him tighter than she had ever hugged him before.

Hannelore and her father did the same only a few yards away.

Darbian stood back watching, happy for the first time in a while.

"Who are you?" said Elizabeth.

"My name is Darbian. I'm a Warden...the last Warden. I'm a guardian of this sector of the universe and friend to the children," Darbian said.

Brendan looked on.

Micah picked his head up. "Darbian saved us from Vinitor and a lot of other things too."

"How did you get involved with Vinitor? Where did you two go that night?" Elizabeth hugged her son all the tighter.

"We were chasing after the dog and the dog changed into Taurean and then Vinitor abducted us. It was a long day!" Micah babbled.

"What on Earth?" Elizabeth said.

"Parents, please know that your children are safe and that they've been a great help, but I must leave now. My work to protect this planet is not complete. Wish me a safe journey. I'm going to need it," Darbian said.

"Take me with you, Darbian," Micah cried.

Darbian looked back and remembered the words that the Timekeeper had spoken to him.

"Take me with you. I want to become a Warden like you. I want to help you defeat Halinkoy. Did you think I would change my mind?" Micah wiped away his tears and stood resolved.

"I don't know what you're talking about, but absolutely not. You just got home; you're not going anywhere!" Elizabeth clapped her hands as if to signal a pet.

"I want the same thing and it's time to stop putting it off," said Hannelore.

"You're staying right here, young lady," said Brendan.

"You don't understand, Dad. He needs us. He's all alone, and the danger is only just getting started. We can't leave him after all we've been through together," Hannelore implored.

"You belong here. I belong up there." Darbian pointed toward the sky.

"No! The Timekeeper said we were to be tested. He knows the future! You don't, Darbian! Please let us come with you!" Micah ran back and hugged Darbian.

Darbian had not been hugged in a very long time. In fact, he couldn't remember the last time it happened.

Hannelore ran up next to him and joined in the hug.

"You come back here, Micah!" cried Elizabeth.

"You said it yourself, Mom! Before I left, you said God would protect us, and God did just that. Darbian rescued us from Vinitor and protected us all along the way." Micah turned to face Darbian. "Now, Darbian's back to protect us from someone even worse. And he needs our help to do it."

"You can't be serious," said Brendan.

"I'm very serious," replied Hannelore.

"It's too dangerous. I love you both, but it's too dangerous." Darbian's eyes welled up. "I'm going to program the Convergence to move the planet. Once I've fought off Aculpus then you will activate it. I have to leave the planet and I have to make sure Aculpus leaves the planet too. When you see Gregorical and I leave the city and then Aculpus follow us, that's when you'll activate it."

Aculpus' ship approached in the distance.

"Aculpus is coming. He'll be here soon. Go now; go with your parents. I must leave you. Goodbye," Darbian said.

"Don't leave, Darbian. Don't leave me like my father did," Micah cried out. "You don't understand. I've already lost my dad. I know what's it like to deal with terrible things. If you leave without us, then we'll never get the chance to make it count for something," screeched Micah.

"Micah, Hannelore...if you leave, you may never see your families again. You'll lose so much more than what you've already lost," replied Darbian.

"You heard the Timekeeper, Darbian. I'm meant for something special. He's been watching me all my life. How will I become what I'm supposed to be unless I go with you?" Micah said.

Darbian looked the boy in the eye. "None of us knows what we're supposed to become, Micah."

"Darbian, I know what I'm supposed to become... someone who matters," Micah said.

"Everyone matters, Micah. You don't have to be a hero. You don't have to save galaxies. You matter because you exist," replied Darbian.

Just then, Aculpus' ship appeared nearby.

The sound of the engine buzzed overhead.

"Time's up, children. I have to fight now. Get away from here. The battle is about to begin," Darbian said.

Aculpus' ship came in close and hovered above the neighborhood.

Aculpus elevated to the top of the ship and appeared out of a hatch. "Prepare to die!"

Darbian and the others looked back to see if Aculpus was about to descend to the ground.

Instead, Aculpus pulled out a laser rifle, aimed it at the children, and fired.

Darbian dove in the way to take the brunt of the weapon fire, but he couldn't absorb all the shots.

Hannelore was struck and fell to the ground.

"Hannelore!" cried her father.

CHAPTER 19

HANNELORE'S FATHER ran toward her broken body. "No! My little girl!"

"Aculpus!" shouted Darbian. "You coward!"

Just then Gregorical came flying in from down the street, used his own lasers to shoot the weapon out of Aculpus's hand, and not so gently nudged Aculpus off the top of his ship and down to the ground. "No weapons," said Gregorical.

Aculpus was shaken and struggled to get up.

Darbian rushed to Hannelore's side. "She's wounded... badly. Micah, come help! Mr. Allbrooks, we have to get her into a stasis pod inside Gregorical's infirmary. And we have to do it now!"

"Tell me what to do," said Brendan.

Micah rushed over. "Is she going to be okay?"

"Gregorical, I need a stasis pod open now!" Darbian kneeled over Hannelore.

Gregorical landed next to Darbian and Hannelore, nearly crushing a nearby house. He opened his bay door.

Darbian picked Hannelore up and rushed her inside.

"Mr. Allbrooks, I need you to stay by her side and do precisely as Gregorical instructs you. There's a battle ahead for me and it must be away from here."

Micah, Brendan, and Elizabeth all followed closely.

Gregorical was equipped with a small infirmary, but only had bare essentials as far as the best medicine available. He opened a tube in the infirmary wall and a stasis pod popped out.

Darbian placed her inside the pod and closed it. "Use lots of Meticulo, Gregorical, lots." Darbian relaxed for a moment against the infirmary wall. He rubbed his face and slunk to the floor.

Micah rushed over to grab Darbian's arm. "Darbian, please tell me she'll be okay. Please tell me that!"

"Micah, I'm not sure. I think we got to her in time, but I'm not a doctor," Darbian responded.

Brendan stood over the stasis pod watching his unconscious girl. "Tell me what to do! How can I help?"

Gregorical responded. "Mr. Allbrooks, first, I want you to calm down."

Brendan jerked his head up towards the ceiling. "My daughter is dying! I will not calm down."

"She's not dying Mr. Allbrooks. Not while I can do something about it." Gregorical retracted the stasis pod back inside the wall.

Brendan put his hands up against a murky window trying to maintain a glimpse of his little girl. "Please, for the love of God, tell me there's something I can do."

"Just watch. When she wakes up, she will want to see you first," Gregorical said.

On the other side of the room, Darbian and Micah were trying not to shed tears.

Micah buried his face in his hands. "I was supposed to look out for her and I couldn't do anything."

"Trouble follows us, Micah, and it always will." Darbian looked down at the boy. "I want you to stay with me, do you understand? I need your help. I need it now and I'll need it in the future. And you need my help. I can't protect you if I'm not with you. Danger will not leave you just because I do."

"I'll do whatever you need me to do," Micah said while crying.

"I need you to program the Convergence. Can you do that?" Darbian said.

"Yes, I think I can if Gregorical helps me," Micah replied.

"He'll help you, Micah. Ask him anything you need to," said Darbian. "For now, I have to face Aculpus, and I promise you he'll be defeated."

"Remember Hannelore," said Micah.

"No trouble there," replied Darbian. He dashed out of the ship and found Aculpus.

Aculpus was just picking himself up off the ground. "Darbian, I was afraid you'd run away."

Darbian raced toward Aculpus and gave him a jab to the jaw. "No such luck for you."

Aculpus fell to the ground and cried out, "Rites of Morolith, Rites of Morolith, let us fight properly."

Darbian backed away. "You're a slimy, cowardly, worthless waste of flesh!"

"Same to you," Aculpus retorted. "But the Rites of Morolith demand a proper arena. I'll meet you in the city center. There's a lovely park there where I can kill you in front of lots of people."

"Be careful what you wish for," replied Darbian.

Aculpus inputted directions on a control pad on his wrist. He sent a command for his ship to lower itself enough for him to jump inside.

The ship lowered itself and Aculpus did a backflip into the bay door.

"Gregorical, I'm coming back. We're going to the city center. I'll fight Aculpus there." Darbian turned back and boarded Gregorical once again.

This time, Elizabeth greeted him at the bay door. "Where are you taking my son?"

"My dear lady, your son is the bravest child I've ever seen. He's going to be a Warden, and I will train him. For now, I need his help. I hope you understand," Darbian replied.

"No, I don't understand. I'm afraid Hannelore may die and I'm afraid my son may be next." Elizabeth shed tears. "Do you have children, Darbian? Do you understand the pain I'm going through? He's all I have left."

Darbian lowered his head and then raised it again. "No, I don't have any children, but I promise to protect Micah as though he were my own. I'll die before I let anything happen to him."

"Did that work for Hannelore?" Elizabeth replied.

Darbian pressed forward. "Hannelore's father is here as well. He needs comfort."

Elizabeth followed Darbian through the corridor. "I'm in no shape to comfort anyone, but I'll try. Why am I even doing this? If my son doesn't come home, then I don't know what I'll do."

Gregorical took off once again and flew toward the city center. They landed and noticed Aculpus was already there.

Aculpus exited his craft and walked up next to a large fountain.

Darbian exited Gregorical and walked until he stood only a few yards from Aculpus.

"The Rites of Morolith are clear," said Aculpus. "We fight with our bare hands...no weapons, no armor, no devices of any kind. The winner has the right to demand whatever he wishes of the loser. You're honor bound to follow these rules, Darbian."

"Don't speak to me of honor. Fight me," replied Darbian.

The two ran at each other.

Remembering that Aculpus had no actual vision, Darbian ducked down and Aculpus missed with his first swing.

Darbian used his leverage to trip up Aculpus from behind. Once he had Aculpus on the ground, Darbian pounded his face hoping to wound his radar-like sense.

Aculpus, the stronger and more experienced fighter of the two, reached up with his legs and grabbed Darbian from behind his head and threw him to the ground.

"I am not so easily injured, Warden," said Aculpus.

* * *

"Gregorical, I can't figure out how to set the Convergence to move Earth. What do I do?" Micah said.

"Micah, have you tried activating the voice command? Most Armankouri technologies have such a feature," Gregorical said.

"Micah, what is this all about?" asked Elizabeth

"Mom, there's no time to explain," Micah moved the Convergence up on a table in the middle of the infirmary.

"What does this thing do?" Elizabeth was quite far behind.

"Mom, we have to move the planet. Halinkoy is coming to destroy it. This is the only way to protect it for now." Micah said.

Elizabeth's ears perked up. "I don't understand. Who is coming? Are you talking about more aliens? Why would they want to destroy us?"

Gregorical spoke up. "Mrs. Alfero, there is a villain, the likes of which this planet has never seen, and he is approaching. That's why we've returned...to protect Earth."

"But you said you're going to move the planet? How could something so small do something like that?" Elizabeth said.

"I really don't know, Mom. The Armankouri invented it. They're really smart; that's all I got," Micah replied.

"Well, where could you possibly move the planet?" Elizabeth said.

"The Convergence will decide for us," said Gregorical.

"What about the other planets? And the sun? What are you going to do about them?" Elizabeth had picked up on a very important fact.

"She's right, Micah, the other planets in this system form a unique balance along with the Earth. They should all move together," said Gregorical.

"One planet at a time, Gregorical. I'm just trying to figure out how to move one," Micah replied.

"Micah, try the large orange button in the center," said Gregorical.

"Ok, hopefully we don't make it move on its own like Taurean did," Micah pushed the large orange button.

A foreign language emanated out from the Convergence. It went on for several minutes.

Micah backed away from the device. "What's it saying Gregorical? Did we do something wrong?"

"No my child. This is an ancient version of the Armankouri native language. The language translation program is stored in my databanks. It is giving us instructions on how to operate the device," replied Gregorical.

Micah nodded his head and smiled. "Awesome!"

"I will speak the correct language now and program it according to the plan." Gregorical spoke the native language of the Armankouri and commanded the Convergence to move the entire solar system to a point and time of the Convergence's choosing.

Micah pulled on his hair. "Is it done?"

"Not yet. First, I need to make sure that Halinkoy's ships don't move with the solar system. For that matter, we can't move either." Gregorical relayed those specifications.

"How about now?" Micah was impatient as though he were waiting for Christmas.

"That's strange. I didn't expect that possibility," Gregorical said.

Micah furrowed his brow. "What's wrong?

"The Convergence works by surrounding itself and every object it's programmed to move with a field of energy. What I've just asked the device to do is create multiple fields for an unknown number of objects inside the primary field thus shielding these various objects from the effects. Anomalies could result." Gregorical displayed a diagram of the energy fields on his main screen.

Elizabeth responded, "English, please."

"The Convergence has informed me there is a possibility of time warp," Gregorical replied.

"Well, what would that mean?" Elizabeth placed her hands on her hips.

"Flashes of light, random wormholes, and a great degree of unpredictability," the machine said.

Micah's mouth hung open. "For who?"

"For us and for any other ship. It's possible we won't remain in our current time and location." Gregorical pondered for a moment. "It's a risk we must take. There are no other options."

"So we may pop out in another time? Or another place?" Micah said. "Well, maybe we could lure the other ships away?"

"Not likely, Micah," Gregorical replied. "We can't know how many ships we're dealing with. That and I doubt Halinkoy will fall for any trick that leads him away from the Earth, even for a moment."

"So we chance it?" The boy said.

"Yes, and I believe our plan will work. All we need now is for someone to activate it manually," said Gregorical.

"Mom, you have to do it," said Micah.

"What? Why me?" Elizabeth said as she rubbed her shoulder.

"I have to leave, Mom. Someone has to be here to use the Convergence. It can't be me. Hannelore's dad is too upset to even think straight right now. It can't be him either. It has to be you." Micah paused. "You can save the world!"

"Mrs. Alfero, all you must do is push the blue button on the side. That will activate the commands that have already been programmed in," said Gregorical.

"I can't let you leave again, Micah. I just got you back." Elizabeth said.

"Mom, I'll be okay. Darbian is going to train me to be a Warden. I'm going to help people. I'm going to be an astronaut...sort of," said Micah.

"No, you're too young to decide that for yourself. You

don't know what you're getting yourself into," Elizabeth replied.

"Mom, please. I've got a chance to do something special...to be something special. Please don't try to stop me." Micah shed a tear.

"You're already someone special to me," said Elizabeth.

Micah shifted from one foot to the other. "I know, but..."

Elizabeth winced. "But what?"

"I always wanted to be like Dad. There's more to life than being safe." Micah clenched his jaw. "Mom, whenever people looked at Dad, they saw him doing something meaningful. Now, I've got that chance."

It had been since before the explosion that Micah had shown any desire to do much of anything. Something in him had been rekindled. He had returned from his slumber and was ready to take on the world again.

"Micah, I love you. I pray God will take care of you some way, somehow." Elizabeth cried.

"So you'll do it?" said Micah as a smile beamed from his face.

"Yes, I'll do it. I'll do whatever the voice...ship thingy is telling me to do," Elizabeth said.

"Actually, my name is Gregorical," he replied.

"Frankly, I don't care, spaceship. I want you to take care of my boy." Elizabeth said.

"Yes, ma'am," replied Gregorical.

* * *

Darbian and Aculpus had been pummeling each other for several minutes.

Aculpus finally gained the upper hand, threw a weakened Darbian to the ground and pounced on him. "Give in, Darbian."

"I would rather die first," replied Darbian.

"You'll receive that wish sooner than later." Aculpus beat Darbian in the face repeatedly. He beat him until Darbian fell unconscious.

Aculpus Atronis had won the fight.

After a few minutes, Darbian slowly woke up. "What happened?"

"You lost, Darbian," said Aculpus. "It was certain I would beat you. You weren't even a worthy opponent. I suppose I didn't train you all that well after all."

"I didn't lose," Darbian said.

"Oh you most certainly did. Try lifting your head if you don't believe me," said Aculpus.

Darbian tried lifting his head, and he was so woozy when doing so he fell back to the ground.

"You're honor bound to give me what I want. You're duty bound. Do you admit this?" Aculpus said.

"Yes, I admit it," replied Darbian.

"Good," said Aculpus. "I want you to give me the Convergence. I know you have it. I overheard you and the humans talking about it earlier as I laid outside the ship."

"Absolutely not," replied Darbian.

"You're honor bound!" cried Aculpus. "Do it and I'll spare your life."

"Why would you want it? You've already used it once, right? You rigged it to work as a Time Bomb and then you detonated it, didn't you?" Darbian said.

"You think you have it figured out, do you? How I was able to make the Wardein disappear, to throw them into a state of nonexistence?" Aculpus laughed.

"That's how you did it, wasn't it? Tell me," Darbian said.

"I won't tell you anything. You, however, are duty bound to give me what I want. Now do as you're told!" Aculpus screamed.

Darbian shifted his leg out from under himself. "What if I promise to trade you something better if you tell me how you made the Wardein disappear? If you did such a good job getting rid of them, then you should have no problem telling me. After all, there's no way I could bring them back, is there?"

"There is nothing better than to control time and space itself. No promises, no more games. You have no right to trade anything. You're bound to give me the Convergence. Now, you'll give it to me or I'll kill your other friends and take it myself," Aculpus said.

"Doesn't it bother you knowing you can't brag about what you've done...how you did it? It looks like Halinkoy will take all the credit for getting rid of the Wardein. Looks like you were just a pawn in his plan," Darbian said.

"Shut up, you piece of filth," Aculpus responded. "I was the one who destroyed the Convergence to create the Time Bomb effect. No one can ever take that away from me," he fumed.

Darbian tipped up his chin towards his opponent. "But it was Halinkoy's idea, wasn't it? That's what it's all about, isn't it? Halinkoy said I was the weakest Warden, and that you were the strongest. So tell me how the strongest Warden was reduced to a henchman in this whole mess?"

Aculpus growled.

Darbian lifted himself up slightly. "Tell me how the big, bad Aculpus Atronis went from a great hero to a miserable lackey."

Aculpus took a few steps closer to Darbian. "Everyone knows now I was the greatest among the Wardein...the most formidable, the most cunning. I defeated them all with a push of a button. That will never be forgotten."

"Everybody already thought you were the greatest. They already knew you were our finest warrior," Darbian said. "But all that time you didn't understand that true significance doesn't come from war. You thought a warrior's value was in destroying. So instead of offering peace, you sought to conquer. I don't buy all this nonsense of a better order and a universe without conflict. No, you don't believe any of that. You did it for yourself, plain and simple. You killed to make yourself feel powerful. You wanted to feel important. All you did was prove you're just a tool in the hands of a madman. That's the thing that people will never forget."

Aculpus paced around Darbian and pointed at him.. "You'll give me what I want now or I'll take it. Order Gregorical to bring it to me and everyone lives. I've already warned you. If you want that other child to live, then you'll give me what I want."

"Are you so cold now?" Darbian shut his eyes for a moment.

"I've done it before, Darbian. I tried to do it earlier, in fact, and may yet be successful," replied Aculpus.

"You're truly lost then. How could a Warden betray his brothers? How could a Warden hurt innocent people? How could a Warden kill a defenseless child? What did you fight for all those years? Why did you dedicate your life to justice? Surely, there must have been something inside you that desired to do good. You risked your life on many occasions to save so many. What happened to you?" Darbian rolled over on his shoulder.

Aculpus spoke so calmly. "Are you going to give me the Convergence or am I going to have to take it from the child's lifeless hands?"

Darbian lifted his communicator up. "Gregorical, I have bad news. I've been defeated by Aculpus. He wants me to give him the Convergence. He's threatening to kill Micah unless I make good on my oath to follow the Rites of Morolith."

"You claim to have honor, Darbian. Follow through with it or be a grand hypocrite like me," said Aculpus.

"Like you, eh?" replied Darbian.

"Yes, and the last thing you want is to be like me, isn't it? What do you say?" Aculpus grinned.

"No," said Darbian. "The rules aren't always what they're cracked up to be."

"No?" replied Aculpus. "You can't say no. You're duty bound!"

"Duty to whom, Aculpus? You got rid of the Wardein. Who will enforce my oath to the Rites of Morolith? No one," said Darbian.

"I'll enforce the Rites. I'll take the Convergence anyway and punish you by killing the child," said Aculpus.

Darbian scoffed. "I know something you don't, Aculpus," He sat up.

"What's that?" replied Aculpus

"I know the future. Micah has a great destiny in store. He must be tested. You won't be able to kill him," said Darbian.

"No one knows the future Darbian. Are you really that foolish? The only thing that matters is power. That's how you craft destiny," replied Aculpus.

"I don't believe that." Darbian wiped his eyes. "There are things happening here than neither you nor I understand. Some things aren't written in stone, some things are."

"You're a babbling fool," replied Aculpus.

"Besides, Micah is aboard Gregorical now." Darbian grimaced and grabbed his head. "You really think you'll defeat Gregorical?"

"Gregorical is a fine machine. In fact, I was a little jealous when he was issued to you. I never thought you deserved him. But he's just a machine. He can be reprogrammed." Aculpus turned and walked away.

Darbian lifted his communicator to his mouth and murmured. "Gregorical, close up your bay, protect everyone inside, but I need you to take off right now. They must deploy the Convergence without me. Furthermore, my old friend, I need you to destroy both Aculpus and I. I'm going to lunge at him and keep him occupied. You finish the job!"

Gregorical took off as Darbian ordered. "Sir, you can't be serious."

"I'm very serious," replied Darbian. "Aculpus will flee to his ship and take off after you. There's no other way to stop him except for you to kill us both while I distract him."

Aculpus was already several meters away by now.

Darbian gasped for air. "No more time." He stood up, ran gingerly, and tackled Aculpus from behind. "Do it now!"

CHAPTER 20

GREGORICAL TOOK a firing posture in the sky

"Do it now, Gregorical! No time to argue!" Darbian said as he wrestled Aculpus to the ground.

Just then, Vinitor's command ship entered the atmosphere above the city.

"Sir," said Gregorical. "Vinitor's ship has arrived."

"Vinitor?" Darbian screamed. "That's the last thing we need right now. How in the world did he break free of the time dilation field?"

Vinitor's ship hurtled toward the Earth's surface.

A message was sent back to Gregorical from the mammoth invader in the sky. "This is Taurean of the Armankouri calling Master Darbian."

Gregorical piped the message through Darbian's communicator.

"Is that who I think it is?" replied Darbian.

"I believe so," Gregorical replied.

"Do you need any assistance, Master Darbian?" Taurean said.

"I need you to bring that ship under control before it

crashes into the Earth!" Darbian grumbled as he struggled with Aculpus.

Aculpus broke free and struck Darbian in the face.

Darbian hit the ground with a thud.

Aculpus wasted no time. He ran for his ship.

"Taurean, you have a tractor beam aboard that ship, don't you? Use it to capture the other ship in the vicinity?" Darbian said.

"My pleasure, Master Darbian. I've already mastered most of the ship's functions. I'm still a bit shaky on piloting, however," Taurean replied.

As Aculpus took off, a tractor beam grabbed his ship out of mid-air and brought it into Vinitor's docking bay.

The trouble was that Taurean was having great difficulty slowing down Vinitor's ship. He wasn't used to piloting such a massive craft, and he was surprised by how the ship's gravity interacted with that of Earth.

"Taurean, please slow that ship down before you crash into the city. That'll cause massive destruction," Darbian said.

"Yes, Master Darbian, I'm trying," Taurean replied.

"There should be an emergency stop function, Taurean. Use it now before you hit the city," Darbian said.

Vinitor's ship was heading toward Garden City at an alarming rate. Within a few seconds, it would crash into the city if it wasn't stopped in its tracks.

"Taurean, now!" Darbian yelled.

Taurean scrambled around the bridge and finally found what was akin to an emergency brake. He pulled the lever with all his strength and it barely moved. "Sir, we may have a problem."

Around the nose of the ship was a wall of fire. The tip was bright red as it barrelled through the atmosphere.

The ship shook as it encroached ever closer to the city.

Taurean was thrown off his feet. "Oh my."

He landed upside down on the brake lever and as he grabbed it, the ship shifted again and it threw his entire weight against the brake.

The lever slid into proper position and locked into place.

The reverse engines thrusted at full power with such a glow that it appeared to be another sun in the sky.

With only a few feet to spare, the ship stopped before it would have struck Garden City's tallest building. Like a missile aimed for the city, the ship protruded from the skyline. There it hovered in the air.

Darbian looked up at the odd placement of the ship. "I suppose that'll do."

Taurean rubbed his shoulder. "Darbian, is everything alright down there?"

"Yes, whatever you did, you did it just in time," replied Darbian.

Taurean laid on the floor of the bridge. "I suppose I can make an entrance, no?"

"Gregorical, come pick me up. I need to speak with the traitor," said Darbian.

Gregorical did as he was asked.

"I need to speak to Taurean too. How in the world did he get out of that time dilation field?" Darbian limped his way up to Gregorical.

Gregorical flew back up to Vinitor's ship and entered through the cargo bay.

Taurean greeted them there.

"Taurean, my friend, I've never been so glad to see an Armankouri in my life," Darbian said.

"Oh Darbian, you kidder. As if you've ever had a negative encounter with an Armankouri," Taurean replied.

Darbian was bruised and bloodied. He walked gingerly towards Taurean. "How did you escape the time dilation field?"

"It's funny you should ask. Long before I left Armankour, my ailing father told me I would meet a Warden, that I would aid him, but that I would be trapped in a time dilation field. Using his clout with the security force, he was able to procure for me an experimental device that counteracted such phenomena. Darbian, that's why I insisted that I be the one to activate the Chrono drive inside Vinitor's ship. I knew I had a chance of withstanding the effects of the time dilation field. And I did," Taurean laughed.

"Your father is Bau Gerean?" Darbian said.

"Yes, Master Darbian, and I've heard all about your little adventure together. And yes, I even heard you've had a few negative encounters with the Armankouri," Taurean said, smiling.

"What did you do with Vinitor? The human hostages?" Darbian said.

"Oh yes, that was simple. I tied up Vinitor and his guards. It took a while, but after a few days I dragged them all into place. Once I moved them into the prison ward, I released the humans. They traded places if you will. In fact, the humans are in one of the cargo bays camping out. There were a few children in there, and if I didn't know better, I would think they were having fun aboard a stolen spaceship," Taurean shrugged.

Darbian hugged him.

"Oh, I'm very glad to see you too, Darbian," Taurean said.

"Hannelore has been hurt. She might die," Darbian said.

"What?" exclaimed Taurean.

Aculpus shot her with a laser rifle.

"That fiend," said Taurean.

"I want to talk to him now. What bay did you pull his ship into?" Darbian said.

"It's in the detention bay and still surrounded by the tractor beam. That villain is a captive audience for now," Taurean said.

"Let's go," Darbian side-stepped Taurean and headed for Aculpus.

"I want to go too," said Micah. "I want to see him and tell him I'll make sure he pays for what he's done to Hannelore."

"Micah, come if you wish, but there will be no vengeance. Revenge is a terrible master. Justice is the way. Aculpus will be punished for what he's done, but it will be according to the law," Darbian said.

"I guess you're the boss," said Micah.

Darbian, Taurean, and Micah walked through the corridors to the detention bay where Aculpus' ship was being held.

There was a visible but transparent shielding around the craft.

Micah knocked on it to see if it would hurt, and it shocked him.

"Don't do that, my boy," Taurean said.

"Aculpus! I need a word with you," yelled Darbian.

Aculpus walked out of his hatch and stood on top of his ship.

"I assume you've already tried to blast your way out of the tractor beam," Darbian said

"You're correct, and I'm now your prisoner. What a turn of events, eh?" Aculpus said.

"How did you get the Convergence in the first place? How did you rig it to become a Time Bomb?" Darbian got right to the point.

"I don't know what you're talking about," replied Aculpus.

"Stop playing games with me. Your days of sabotage are over. You're imprisoned now and you'll be brought to justice," Darbian responded.

"I'll not face justice," Aculpus said. "Soon Halinkoy will be here to destroy this planet and he'll take me with him."

"No shock there. Halinkoy himself told me he was coming, but we have a way to defeat him," said Darbian.

"A lot has happened since I've been gone, I see," said Taurean.

"Defeat Halinkoy?" Aculpus laughed. "You're out of your mind. Perhaps I beat you too harshly."

"How did you get possession of the Convergence?" Darbian thrust his finger towards the floor.

"It doesn't matter now. What's done is done," replied Aculpus.

Gregorical buzzed Darbian. "Sir, Halinkoy's ships are in orbit. The same three we encountered above Crystal Dawn. We must enact the plan soon."

"I guess we're taking you with us as our prisoner," Darbian said. "Taurean, we'll need you to get this ship back into orbit."

"Right," said Taurean.

Sounds of thunder echoed through the corridors of the ship.

Halinkoy's forces had fired on the Earth far sooner than Darbian anticipated.

"That's a bad sign," said Darbian.

"What?" exclaimed Aculpus. He ran back inside his ship and initiated a communication with Halinkoy. "Supreme One, I'm still on Earth. Please don't fire on it yet!"

Halinkoy responded. "Were you able to kill Darbian and the children?"

Aculpus grabbed one set of ears and rubbed them ever so gently. "No, my Supreme One, I haven't been able to do that yet."

"Then you're of no use to me," replied Halinkoy. "I gave you the chance to have real power, Aculpus. I showed you a better way to bring order and peace, but you've repaid me with failure. You've proven yourself unworthy. We'll continue with the destruction of the planet. So go all who defy me!"

The communication ended.

Aculpus exited his ship with sunk shoulders.

Darbian stared down Aculpus. "He doesn't care does he? He wants to destroy the planet now, and he's going to do it whether you, his alleged servant, are still here or not. Isn't that right?"

"Please let me go before the Earth breaks up. Don't force me to stay. Please remember my good deeds down through the years. Certainly they're worth something?" Aculpus said.

"Your good deeds are worth nothing if not done for the right reasons. You did them for selfish reasons. It doesn't matter though; you won't die on this planet. We're moving it with the Convergence and Taurean is going to take this ship away from here...with you in it," Darbian said.

The blasts continued in the distance as Halinkoy fired upon the planet.

Darbian turned to walk away.

"I'll bargain with you," said Aculpus.

Darbian's eyes straightened. "Absolutely not," he replied. "Gregorical, it's time to move ahead with the plan. Go back to the surface and leave the Convergence to be activated. Micah and Hannelore will come with us. I will stay with Taurean for the moment. I'll meet you in orbit to face Halinkoy."

"What about the people on this ship, the hostages?" Aculpus mumbled.

Darbian threw his hands up. "The hostages! Somehow I forgot them." He beat the wall.

Meanwhile, more blasts impacted the Earth's surface.

"Let me help you, Darbian. I'll help you get the hostages out," said Aculpus.

Darbian turned back to Aculpus. "Why would you do that?"

"It works perfectly, Darbian. The Rites of Morolith, you never gave me what I asked for. I've changed my mind; I want a trade. You give me my freedom and I'll fly out into orbit and distract Halinkoy's ship. He left me to die. I have no more loyalty to him," Aculpus said.

"A trade? How do I know you'll keep your word?" Darbian said.

"You wanted so badly to keep your honor, Darbian. I saw it in your eyes. You hated not granting my request. You refused because you think I'm evil. Well, you're right; I am evil. This way, though, you get your honor, and I get my freedom. The people are safe and you'll never see me again," Aculpus said.

"You didn't answer my question!" Darbian smacked the wall.

The blasts came again and again.

"I'll give you information. You want me to show you I have no loyalty to Halinkoy? Then I'll tell you this. The boy's father is still alive. He's in stasis aboard Halinkoy's flagship. He's not far from us right now as a matter of fact," Aculpus said.

Darbian narrowed his eyes.

"Halinkoy is distracted every time he sees the boy. His mind plays with him because Micah's father is a part of him now. There's your proof, Darbian. That's how you know I'll keep my word because I've just given you the key to defeat Halinkoy," Aculpus pounded the shielding.

"What? That's not possible!" Micah rubbed his forehead.

"Halinkoy didn't tell me how he did it. He only told me never to tell you the truth. In fact, he wanted me to kill all of you, and because I failed, he has betrayed me," Aculpus said.

Micah rushed up to the shielding. "You're just lying to save yourself!"

"I don't think he is, Micah. No, I don't think he is," said Darbian. "A little faith in time of trouble."

"I thought you didn't believe in faith," said Micah.

The blasts continued to rain down upon the Earth. The rumbles of earthquakes were heard in the distance.

"Time to move, Aculpus. I'm going to let you out, and you'll distract Halinkoy long enough for us to get these people to safety," Darbian said.

"You can't be serious," said Micah. "I don't believe him!"

"We have to take the chance, my child. Justice will have to wait," said Darbian as he released the shielding. "Go now, Aculpus. Do one last good thing."

Aculpus ran back into his ship and took off.

"Darbian, what if it's not true? What if my dad is dead and Aculpus is lying just to save his own skin?" Micah said with tears in his eyes.

"My boy, I never told you my suspicion, but remember when Halinkoy was so unsettled when he saw you on Crystal Dawn. Do you remember? Do you remember that he recognized you? This is the only way that was possible. Someone you know is inside Halinkoy's head and somehow, I don't understand how it could have happened, but somehow your father survived and is there inside Halinkoy's mind," Darbian said. "I need you to trust me, my boy."

Taurean piped back in. "Master Darbian, where shall I take the ship once it's in orbit? Where will we meet?"

"Taurean, we should meet at the Belt of Orion, our old stomping grounds. But that has to wait because we need to get the people off the ship," Darbian spoke into his communicator.

"Oh dear, you're correct! How could I have been so clumsy?" Taurean responded.

* * *

Aculpus' ship exited Earth's atmosphere and came face to face with Halinkoy's flagship.

"This is Aculpus Atronis, calling the Supreme One. Please respond," said Aculpus.

Halinkoy opened a new communication with Aculpus. "My servant, you've escaped. Good for you. Perhaps I was too quick to pronounce you unworthy. Now bask in the glory of the destruction of this planet."

"Wait, my Supreme One. Cease fire, please. There's something you don't know. The Convergence is on Earth and Darbian plans to use it to move the planet to a secure location," Aculpus replied.

"What?" Halinkoy recoiled. "Cease fire on the planet. I want an expeditionary force to go down to the surface immediately. Zero in on Garden City and find the Convergence. We must recover the device!"

The ships stopped firing and, for now, the planet Earth was safe from destruction.

Tammeder soldiers left the bridge of Halinkoy's flagship just as they were commanded.

"Thank you, Aculpus. You've served me well and for that you'll be rewarded," Halinkoy said.

"A reward? That sounds wonderful!" Aculpus said.

"I plan on making you the chief of my new security force. You already have so much experience in war from your time as a Warden. I suspect you would enjoy enforcing my law, good law for a change," Halinkoy said.

"Excellent, I'll go back to my work of destroying the old Wardein bases and return to you when I'm finished," Aculpus said.

"No, I want you to stay here. I'll need your help to destroy Darbian if the Tammeder soldiers aren't effective," Halinkoy replied.

"Yes, I would enjoy that," replied Aculpus.

CHAPTER 21

"THE SHIPS STOPPED FIRING!" Darbian said. He clasped his hands as if to say thanks.

Taurean piped back in. "Darbian, where should I set the ship? The city sprawls for miles all around. Do we have time to move it to the countryside?"

"Taurean, can we reverse the tractor beam and set the people in the middle of the city?" Darbian replied.

"Yes, brilliant! That's exactly what we'll do," Taurean adjusted the controls of the tractor beam.

Darbian and Micah ran for the cargo bay where the hostages were.

Darbian burst through the door. "Attention! Attention everyone! You're about to go back home!"

The crowd of hundreds cheered.

"We need you to proceed in a line to the central holding room. From there, a tractor beam will take you in groups back down to the planet. Just as you came into the ship, you'll go back down to Earth," Darbian said.

"Who are you?" one man asked.

"I'm no one special," said Darbian. "I'm just a person trying to help."

"A hero is what you are," said a woman nearby.

"Well, don't get ahead of yourself ma'am. There's still a lot of trouble ahead," said Darbian.

"Well, I feel better knowing you're here to protect us," said the woman.

"No time for weakness here. These people need me," Darbian said under his breath.

The hostages left the cargo bay.

Darbian and Micah led the crowds down the corridors to the main holding room in the center of the ship. From there, they herded the people into groups of ten and, group by group, used the tractor beam to levitate them back down to the planet

"This is what it's normally like being a Warden, my boy," said Darbian.

"I could get used to that," said Micah.

"Micah, you did set the Convergence to go off remotely, didn't you? How much time did you allow?" Darbian said.

"It's okay, Darbian. My mother's going to do it when we give her the signal," replied Micah.

Darbian gulped. "Does she know how to activate it?"

"She told me she did. I mean, she was a teacher at the Star Force Academy. She should be able to figure it out," said Micah.

Darbian smiled. "Okay then. That should work. Aculpus won't be able to stall much longer though. We have to put the plan into place soon," he said. "Gregorical, have you brought the Convergence back down to Earth?"

"Yes, sir, I landed a moment ago, but I'm having trouble getting Hannelore's father to leave. He wants to be by his daughter's side," Gregorical responded.

"I can understand that. Come back up and get me Gregorical. I'll speak to him. Be quick about it, friend; we don't have much time," Darbian said.

"We have another issue, sir. There appear to be raiding ships coming in from orbit. It's likely they're Tammeder soldiers. If my strategic programming is working correctly, I would say they're coming here to obtain the Convergence," Gregorical said.

Darbian paused and closed his eyes for a moment. "And so this is how it ends...where it began and for the very reason it began. We've come full circle, Micah. The fight for the Convergence decides it all. We must protect Earth at all costs and we must not allow the Convergence to fall into Halinkoy's hands," he said.

"What do we do this time, Darbian?" Micah said.

"We finish this once and for all," replied Darbian.

* * *

Gregorical sat on the ground and opened his bay door to allow Elizabeth to leave with the Convergence.

"Elizabeth, my dear lady, take one of the communicators. They're hanging up on my wall," said Gregorical.

"Thank you, spaceship, or whatever you're called," said Elizabeth. She grabbed one of the communicators and strapped it around her wrist.

"When Darbian gives you the signal, then you are to push the blue button on the side. He won't give you the signal until all the starships have left the planet. Please be patient and don't be tempted to push the button if there's conflict in the air. Now, hide yourself and wait for the signal," Gregorical said.

"You don't have to worry about me, spaceship. I come from good stock!" Elizabeth said.

"Yes, ma'am," replied Gregorical.

Elizabeth looked back at Brendan. "Are you coming? I'm sorry, we've been neighbors all this time and I don't even know your name."

"My name is Brendan," said Hannelore's father. "And no, I'm not coming until she's well. I don't care what happens to me."

"Let these people do their work. They will take care of Hannelore," said Elizabeth.

Brendan turned around and his lip quivered. "I can't leave her."

"Sir, I assure you we will get your daughter the best medical care that the universe can provide. For now, she must come with us," said Gregorical.

"So you'll bring her back to me then? Good as new?" asked Brendan.

"I cannot promise we will be back, sir. We are going to move the planet Earth and it is possible we may never return," Gregorical said.

"Then I won't leave her," said Brendan. "I can't bear the thought of never seeing my little girl again."

"Sir, you have a family here to take care of, do you not?" Gregorical implored.

"No, my wife left a long time ago. Hannelore is all I have," said Brendan.

Gregorical was silent for a moment. "I promise you I will lay my life down to protect your daughter. She will never leave my sensors."

"Promise me you'll bring her back to me! Promise me that," said Brendan.

"I cannot promise you that, sir. I am just a spaceship,

and I have to take orders. There are still battles yet to fight in the cosmos. I am not sure if we will ever be able to return," Gregorical replied.

"You're more than a spaceship. You're a mind. You're an incredible thing and you can promise me anything you want to, but I want you to promise me what is right. Bring back my little girl," Brendan said.

"Okay then, I promise to search for this planet and bring Hannelore back. You will see each other again," Gregorical said.

"Thank you." With that, Brendan left the ship and helped Elizabeth return to her home.

Gregorical took off to meet Darbian and Micah once again.

* * *

The Tammeder ships were inbound and brought with them new terrors. They were oval shaped pods and looked bulky, but glided through the air with ease.

Darbian looked out and saw the ships approaching.

Just then, Gregorical arrived at the docking bay of Vinitor's ship.

"I was fearing we wouldn't see each other for a while," said Darbian. "Where's Hannelore's father?"

"We were able to talk him into leaving. I may or may not have made promises I can't keep," Gregorical replied.

"I don't suppose it matters. Whatever you told him, it was for his own good," Darbian replied.

Gregorical responded, "I'm still programmed with a conscience. I didn't lie. Perhaps one day I will be capable of fulfilling my word."

Micah popped back around the corner and into the

docking bay. "Gregorical, did you give my mother a communicator?"

"Of course," replied the machine.

"Great. It's not as though I'll never see her again, but I wanted to tell her goodbye this time," Micah said.

Darbian and Micah boarded Gregorical, and they took off from Vinitor's ship.

Darbian looked down at Micah. "My boy, it's possible you may never see your mother again."

"I know we said we would never come back, and that it was too dangerous to know where the Earth was, but we have to bring my father back. Now that we know he's out there. We have to rescue him and bring him back to my mother. They need each other," said Micah. "We will do that, won't we?"

"You humans are sentimental creatures. Yes, we're going to rescue your father and everyone else Halinkoy has captured," said Darbian.

"Promise me we'll look for the Earth. Promise me we'll find it again," said Micah.

"I can't promise that, Micah. We must keep the Earth safe and if that means staying away from it, then that's what it means. Be wise, my boy, be wise," said Darbian.

Taurean piped in from his new position on the bridge of Vinitor's ship. "Master Darbian, shall we take off and meet Halinkoy?

"Yes, we shall," replied Darbian. "I'm ready to ruin his day."

Taurean, piloting the mammoth ship, left the skies above Garden City.

Gregorical and Taurean arrived in orbit one after the other. Within a matter of seconds, the Tammeder ships were upon them and opened fire.

"Taurean, I know your people are pacifist so I give you full permission to abandon us and head for safety. We'll be safe. Gregorical's evasive maneuvers are better than any other living thing in the universe...at least in my estimation," Darbian said.

"Are you sure about that, Darbian? I don't want to leave you in trouble," said Taurean.

"Trust me," said Darbian. "We'll be fine."

Taurean stiffened his back. "May we meet again." He set a course for the Belt of Orion and left the system.

The Tammeder ships didn't follow.

"Alright then, time to mess with Halinkoy's head!" Darbian said. He contacted Halinkoy's ship and requested a communication.

Halinkoy responded and looked Darbian in the eye for the first time since their meeting on Crystal Dawn.

"Halinkoy, you sorry excuse for a supreme being. Do your worst!" said Darbian.

"I would, but I will get Aculpus Atronis to do it for me," replied Halinkoy. "Aculpus, you have your second chance to destroy Darbian and his young protege. My Tammeder soldiers haven't been able to catch the Warden. His ship is too evasive, however, your ship can catch him and engage in a winning fight. Do your duty."

Aculpus appeared on the communication. "Yes Supreme One, I'll do my duty."

Darbian wondered if Aculpus had betrayed him once again. He thought that Aculpus should have been gone by now, but realized that he did, just as promised, distract Halinkoy from destroying the Earth.

Aculpus engaged the controls of his ship. "My duty is to fulfill my oath to the Rites of Morolith. I'm honor bound to do so. I've traded aid to Darbian for my freedom. Goodbye

Halinkoy; you're an unworthy arbiter of justice. You punished me despite my faithful service. Now, I go to seek another way and to leave you to your fate."

"You filth!" Halinkoy opened his globe.

Aculpus' ship zipped past the Tammeder fleet and into the depths of space.

"Don't worry about him metal head," Darbian said. "And for that matter, don't worry about me. I may be the last Warden, but that's not important right now. There's a boy you need to talk to."

"It won't work this time Warden. I've made improvements," Halinkoy stuck his nose in the air.

Darbian dipped his head and smirked. "No, there's a human being inside your head...and he loves his son. And there's something about these humans and their sentimentality. It's something even untold brilliance can't overcome."

Halinkoy focused his gaze on Darbian. "This planet is about to die and you with it."

Darbian looked to Micah. "Talk to your dad, my boy. I'm sure he's listening."

Micah walked into view. "Dad, are you in there?"

Halinkoy saw the boy and struggled to maintain his composure. He waved his hands profusely.

"Dad, we're coming to rescue you. We're going to bring you back home so you can see mom again, but right now I need your help." Micah opened his palm and reached toward the screen.

Halinkoy dropped to his knees and moaned in pain. "Fire on the planet! Destroy the planet! Destroy the planet and everything in the path!"

A Tammeder solider swung around from his post. "Supreme One, what about the expeditionary force?"

"Fire on everything!" Halinkoy gripped his head.

Halinkoy's ships fired on the planet once again; however, this time, the Tammeder pods were in the line of fire. One by one, they were destroyed as they absorbed most of the firepower of the battle ships.

Gregorical evaded every single blast.

"Elizabeth," Darbian spoke into his communicator. "It's time, my lady. Activate the Convergence!"

"Goodbye, Mom! I'll see you again someday," said Micah.

Back on Earth, Elizabeth heard the cry of Darbian and the farewells of her only son. "Goodbye Micah. Goodbye Darbian. Goodbye spaceship. Godspeed to you all." She pressed the blue button on the side of the Convergence.

Instantly, a bright blue light encircled the planet. It jumped to the moon and encircled it. The light traveled in every direction and consumed every planet, every moon, every asteroid, every comet, and even the sun itself. Within the time it takes for the glimmer of a star to shine down on a planet, the entire solar system disappeared.

The only things left in place were the Tammeder fleet along with Gregorical and his tiny crew.

"What did you do Darbian?" cried Halinkoy. "What did you do? Where did it go?

Darbian threw his arms up. "That's the beauty of the plan, Halinkoy. I don't know where it went."

Halinkoy slammed his fist on the console in front of him and sparks flew as it cracked in half. "Blow them out of the sky!"

In the very next instant, bright flashes consumed the space around each ship.

The light was so intense that not a soul kept from covering his eyes.

One large, vibrating wormhole appeared behind Halinkoy's ships.

Each of the craft were sucked into the wormhole with such ferocity that a simple kite would have had a better chance of escaping a tornado.

Another wormhole appeared behind Gregorical.

He and his crew were swallowed up all the same.

Each wormhole closed and flashes of light leapt through the empty space like a lightning bolt traveling from cloud to cloud.

"Sir, we have a problem," said Gregorical.

Darbian's knees went weak. "What in the blazes is happening?"

"None of my sensors are reading anything sir. I would guess that..." Gregorical's speech became garbled.

"Gregorical, are you there?" Darbian cried.

There was no response.

* * *

The Earth and the entire solar system reappeared in a far-flung portion of the universe, but on the surface below, the people were taking stock of the attack they had just suffered.

In the middle of Garden City, a military convoy drove up close to the old Palace Hotel. They stopped as soon as they approached a cordoned off area.

A solider approached the door of one of the trucks, gripped the handle, and opened it. "Colonel Russell, sir." He saluted.

"What exactly did we find here?" said Colonel Russell.

"We're not sure what it is, but we think it broke off from one of the spaceships flying around the city. We think it's been here since last week when the initial invasion by Vinitor occurred," the soldier said.

The two walked a few yards until they were forced to squeeze into an alleyway. There they looked over a large hunk of white metal.

"Why did it take us so long to find it?" Colonel Russell asked.

"Sir, it moved," the solider said.

"Moved? Well, who moved it?" Colonel Russell tensed his shoulders. "Are they contaminated in any way?"

"No sir, it moved on its own," the soldier said.

"What?" exclaimed Colonel Russell.

"Traffic cameras confirmed that, sir. Not only that, but ever since we initially observed it earlier today...well, it's been growing."

"Growing? What in the blazes is this thing?" Colonel Russell said as he took a step away.

"I was speaking to Dr. Hendrickson earlier, and she thinks we can reverse engineer it," the solider said.

Colonel Russell "But can we weaponize it?"

"Yes, we think we can," said Dr. Hendrickson as she approached from behind.

"Good, it's high time the aliens, whoever they are, stop fighting over our planet like a child's toy. Thousands around the world are dead from today's attack...whole cities leveled." Colonel Russell became more gruff with every word.

"We need a game changer," said Dr. Hendrickson

"We need to be ready to fight back," said Colonel Russell.

To Be Continued...

THANK YOU!

If you enjoyed the book then please consider leaving a review on Amazon and/or Goodreads.

I sincerely hope you did enjoy it and I'd like to thank you for your purchase!

The Accidental Astronaut represents the first installment in the Among the Stars series. The second installment will be published soon! *Among the Stars: The Midnight Plot* will be available on Amazon! If you want to keep up with the release schedule then follow me over at https://www.matthewkwyers.com

THANK YOU AGAIN!

ABOUT THE AUTHOR

A lifelong fan of speculative fiction, Matthew K. Wyers decided one day to put his overactive imagination to work. He has focused on middle grade fiction because he wants to inspire young people to see the good in the world and in turn embody that goodness so they can positively influence the world around them.

That's why he writes about classic battles between good and evil. The children need to understand that darkness cannot overcome light, and so they have a choice to make in their own lives. Will they wallow in the darkness or shine a light?

Known to his friends simply as Matt, he is a native of Tuscaloosa, Alabama. There you can find him cheering on the Crimson Tide, exploring country roads, or eating lots of Mexican food.

facebook.com/matthewkwyers

twitter.com/matthewkwyers

instagram.com/matthewkwyers

amazon.com/author/matthewkwyers

pinterest.com/matthewkwyers